EPITAPH

To Ens. Steve
Best wishes and
Good luck!

Other books by D. Clayton Meadows

OF ICE AND STEEL

EPITAPH

D. Clayton Meadows

Published by Big River Press
P. O. Box 371, Clallam Bay, Washington 98326
http://www.bigriverpress.com

This is a work of fiction. Tactics described in this work in no way reflect actual tactics used by Navies of the United States, Russia, or any nation. Descriptions of ships, aircraft, weapons and weapon systems, weapon operations or limitations are modified to protect sensitive information. All places, characters and events portrayed in this novel are either fictitious or are used fictitiously. Any resemblance of the characters in this novel to real persons, living or dead, is purely coincidental.

ISBN-13: 978-0-9798744-4-4
ISBN-10: 0-9798744-4-0

Library of Congress Control Number: 2009923441

Printed in the United States of America

First Edition - Trade Paperback printed on acid free paper

Front Image Credit: Steve Neiil
Cover Design: Big River Press

First published 2007 by Aardvark Global Publishing
as a Kindle Advance Reading digital edition
ISBN: 978-1-4276-2900-5

Dedication

For Susan

This book is dedicated to the memory of Commander Phillip Murphy-Sweet. My supply Officer on USS DALLAS SSN 700. Killed in Iraq by a roadside bomb.

EPITAPH

Acknowledgments

When I wrote OF ICE AND STEEL, I found myself with characters that fans of the book wanted to know more about. Unfortunately, I could not seem to find these folks any meaningful employment.

Mr. David Merriman came to the rescue when he suggested the basis for EPITAPH. David is a master model builder, whose contributions to the Submarine Service are beyond measure. He would be upset if I told you what a fine person he is, so I won't.

Steve Neiil, whose art you see on the covers of this book and OF ICE AND STEEL is a talented artist in so many fields. However, his talent is no match for the kindness in his heart.

Thanks to Mr. Brian Stark, whose encouragement and support played no small role in completing EPITAPH.

Mr. Wayne Frey was an invaluable resource. This man knows more about Russian submarines than most Russians do.

To my wife Susan and my boys, Donnie and Andrew, a big thank you for your understanding and patience with me. Soon, my boys will set out on their voyages. I already miss them coming to the office where I write, to ask questions about homework, or to share what is going on in their lives.

This book would have never been worth the paper it was printed on had it not been for my editor and friend, Donna Peerce. Her patience is without measure.

Without the help and understanding of David and Rebecca Brown of Big River Press you would not be reading this book. Their support, patience and willingness to keep me out of trouble gave me hope and drove me on.

I could have never written EPITAPH without the encouragement of you, the readers. I never thought OF ICE AND STEEL would gain the following it has. I only hope you enjoy this one as much.

Thank you to all the men and women of THE UNITED STATES SUBMARINE SERVICE. I do indeed sleep better at night knowing that somewhere in the deep oceans of the world these dedicated and professional Sailors are on constant watch.

EPITAPH

"...*The Events of October 1962 indicated, as they have all through history, that the control of the sea means security. Control of the seas may mean peace. Control of the seas will mean victory. The United States must control the sea if it is to protect your security...*"

~President John F. Kennedy onboard the USS KITTY HAWK

"*Nuclear catastrophe was hanging by a thread ... and we weren't counting days or hours, but minutes.*"

~Soviet General and Army Chief of Operations, Anatoly Gribkov during the Cuban Missile Crisis

"*There is a great streak of violence in every human being. If it is not channeled and understood, it will break out in war or in madness.*"

~Sam Peckinpah

"*The man who strikes first admits that his ideas have given out.*"

~Chinese Proverb

PROLOGUE

"There is a time to take counsel of your fears, and there is a time to never listen to any fear."
~George S. Patton

United States Naval Submarine Base
Groton, Connecticut
January 7th

Grant McKinnon stood alone. Sub-zero gusts blustered and fussed around him as bitter air licked his face. McKinnon's eyes remained fixed; he looked, but did not see.

Pole lamps in the near empty car lot swayed in the angry gale. Though mid-morning, the lamps still shone tired yellow bulbs in a vain attempt to illuminate the furious gray air.

Past McKinnon, figures blurred by a glacial-like vapor of snow and ice hurried as fast as traction would allow. Sailors and civilians alike trudged through muddied frozen slush toward nearby buildings, searching for warmth. Gloved hands held fast to hats or gathered jackets around the owners' bodies. This winter had been bad and this storm was by far the worst.

McKinnon's mind erased much of the early morning. Gone was the memory of the bagel and coffee he'd had for breakfast. The dangerous drive over ice coated roads was now only a blur. With his mind closed little registered in his brain except for the phone call.

It was now three months since the encounter with the German U-boat. Life had almost returned to normal. World attention had gone on, finally focusing on events other than the U-boat. As winter came hard to New England, life was just that, life. McKinnon's had taken an unexpected but wonderful turn, until this morning.

As for the other players in that drama, McKinnon knew little. Becker now lived in Florida and shied away from the media. Requests from magazines, television stations, all went answered. The one time U-boat Commander tried to catch up on almost sixty years of history and progress. Each day his wife Ada required more care. She was feisty as ever, but unlike him, the years had taken their toll.

Carl Blevins was back at his home on the hill, somewhat embarrassed by all the fuss. The retired Chief had done well for himself. The Navy was always quick to latch on to any good public relations opportunity and Carl Blevins proved to be a perfect spokesman.

Then there was Captain First Rank Valerik Danyankov, Commander of the AKULA Class Attack Submarine K-157 VEPR. McKinnon attended the Russian's wedding, but they had had little chance to talk since then. Until this morning.

How did he get my number? Was it really him? Was this all another bad dream? A chill washed over him, though not from the storm. *How can I keep this a secret? What can I do?* There were options, but the results were all bad. McKinnon turned his head. He stared at the hill opposite the bleak empty road. At the top, hidden by the storm, McKinnon wondered if Admiral Burke Tarrent was in his office.

McKinnon reasoned with himself, tried to force himself up the hill, while another part of his mind screamed. He felt his shoulders slump as his mind gave into hopelessness.

Slowly, he turned back. The wind shifted slightly and he could see the waterfront. Nine submarines rested at their berths, as the winter storm frenzied around them. USS PROVIDENCE was closest. Small sheets of ice attached themselves to her rudder, and grew larger as other slabs of thin ice collided and broke apart before again freezing.

Next was USS SEAWOLF, her deadly sleek form rose from the gloom of the river, as ripples of not yet frozen water surged around her.

On the next pier, McKinnon's own USS

MIAMI SSN 755 floated, unmoving as if challenging the weather that swarmed around her. McKinnon looked down on his submarine. Fog and mist wrapped around the silent, black hull, bounced and spewed as it struck the square box-like sail. For the first time he could remember, McKinnon thought the submarine looked somehow evil.

His head turned, his eyes following the barely visible opposite shore of the Thames River. On a clear day, he could have seen the outline of the one time whaling town of New London.

Beyond would be Long Island Sound. Along the same line of site was New York City.

When it happens, will someone on this spot see the mushroom cloud?

Chapter One

THE CAGE

"He who fights with monsters
should be careful lest he
hereby become a monster."
~Friedrich Nietzsche

Persian Gulf
23 Miles from the Iranian Naval Base
Bandar-E Abbas
November 19th

Two meters over a narrow shelf of sand and rock, the small submarine slid through the warm sea.

Rays of sunlight filtered through the clear ocean, and danced along her squat, stubby shape. Ribbons of reflection camouflaged her long rectangular sail, and blended her blunt bow with the water that flowed past. At the ungracious stern, the five-bladed screw turned lazily as it moved her forward.

No more than a meter above her sail, the Persian Gulf's smooth surface gave no hint of the steel beast that swam below.

In the command center of the Iranian submarine, SIMCER, only the faint glow of instruments managed to erode the sticky, ink-like interior. Commander Asha Feroz stood fiercely in the hot humid darkness, his face illuminated in the greenish glow of the passive sonar repeater.

Feroz resembled the Russian built KILO class submarine he commanded. Like her, he was short, just shy of five-and-half feet. In build, he also matched SIMCER. His stout chest and powerful thick arms stretched at the buff colored material of his at-sea tunic.

His face was lighter than most Persians, though his shorn hair was dark black. The face perfectly matched the rest of the Iranian commander : purposeful, and powerfully built.

Only the scar marred the perfect image. The three-decade old injury formed a ragged line of deep angry rouge, with stipples of purple that cut from the forehead, across the brow, down the left side of the nose along the cheek. At the underside of the jaw, the wound bubbled in a waxy red tinted knot. From under the knot, the line of tortured flesh continued down the neck finally ending as it touched his right shoulder. The ghastly wound was but a marker of the damage to his soul.

"Targets?" Feroz hissed from scarred vocal

cords.

"The destroyer remains on course, no indication we've been detected," replied the Sonar Officer.

"And the carrier? Do we still hold her?"

There was a pause as the Sonar Officer checked the KILO's passive sonar screen for the faint throb of the American carrier's huge screws.

"She's there."

"Good," Feroz whispered. "Shallow water has confused their sonar. Even if they hear us, a weapon launch against us would be impossible."

Tension hung like a cloud in the small control room; it wafted up and mixed with the dank humid air.

"Range to Point Echo?" Feroz demanded.

"Three minutes." Came the hushed reply.

"The American Navy thinks we could not make it past them to open water," Feroz growled. "Today we prove them wrong. They will see the Gulf is no cage. At Point Echo, we will turn and fire on the destroyer with three torpedoes. Once it is hit, we run at flank speed for a firing position on the carrier."

The hum of the electronics hid the gasps that came from the darkened faces in the command center.

A minute later, SIMCER slowed to 3 knots. With only a faint swish of hydraulic power, the thin attack periscope pierced the calm surface. As a thin sheet of water fell away, Feroz could clearly see the sleek deadly lines of the destroyer USS CHURCHILL, cutting neatly through the still water, roughly parallel to his own course.

He increased the magnification on the scope's optics and moved the crosshairs aft of the destroyer. Just visible was the control tower of the aircraft carrier USS RONALD REAGAN.

Even from this range, the huge American ship rose like a steel island. Feroz's lip curled in disgust at the sight. His hands tightened on the periscope handles. "Ronald Reagan," he whispered. "How very ironic."

Over the electronic hum, a spring-wound clock mounted over the Fire Control computer, ticked. To those in the command center, the ticks grew louder, as the seconds came and went until the sound was as if a great hammer pounded the two-inch thick hull plates.

"Point Echo." Announced the Navigator.

"Left full rudder." Feroz ordered. Like a dancer, SIMCER's commander gracefully rotated the scope in a quick circle. "Match bearings on target one."

The shallow sea's surface was empty except for Feroz's prey.

"Steady 178." He barked as the submarine aimed her blunted bow to the enemy.

In the crosshairs of the periscope, as the sleek American man-o-war grew larger, the range decreased.

Then Feroz saw the calm ripples of the quiet

sea begin to shiver and whip to foam.

"Helicopter." The Sonar Officer screamed.

Feroz jumped back from the scope as an American SH60B slid like a giant insect into the window of the periscope.

"Captain, ESM detects APS-124 radar from the American helicopter. It's in attack frequency." The young voice cracked.

Trembling with rage, Feroz stepped to the scope again. The helicopter hovered not three meters over the water and ten meters in front of his slowly moving submarine.

Now the Americans were with the advantage. Feroz's eyes went to the two deadly looking Mk-50 torpedoes slung like fangs under SEAHAWK's airframe. Dropped from low altitude, the light yet powerful weapons would acquire his submarine as soon as they hit the water. Seconds later, the fifty-pound shaped charge warheads would blast his tiny KILO into chunks of worthless steel and torn flesh.

The shallow water that just moments before had been her shield, was now a curse. There was nowhere to move, no deep water to hide in. Checkmate.

Then he looked up.

The grinning helicopter pilot waved mockingly. The co-pilot had his head down and was writing. When he held up a white board with black lettering, Feroz's blood boiled. His English was good, and the message clear:

YOUR MOVE BUTT FACE

Feroz's eyes glowed with hate, and shone white in the hot dark command center.

The sound of the beating ASW helicopter's rotors surrounded the KILO's hull and echoed like the drumbeat of an execution. It made some in the command center pant loudly as fear coiled around them.

"Surface!" Feroz howled. "This training exercise is over. Helm, right full rudder, come to course 082. Get us back to our own waters."

SIMCER's blunted bow shattered the calm water as she pressed herself to the surface. As if irritated, she shook herself free of the ocean. Foam spewed from the limber holes along her side as her ballast tanks emptied.

The American helicopter retreated to 500 meters astern, before it turned and vanished as suddenly as it had appeared.

Now stable on the surface, the diesels grumbled to life. Atmosphere control equipment was re-energized. Desperately needed cool, fresh air circulated over sweat-drenched bodies.

Commander Feroz's steps were heavy as he climbed to the bridge. He let his eyes adjust to the bright sunlight before turning his head. The American destroyer was no more than 1000 meters off the port quarter. The slight wave that reared at her bow seemed to sneer at him.

"Someday." He hissed.

Little did he know how soon that would be.

Chapter Two

ORDERS

"Only on paper has humanity yet achieved glory, beauty, truth, knowledge, virtue, and abiding love."
~George Bernard Shaw

Lapadnaya Lista
Russian Submarine Base
December 19th

Her knee-high boots crunched through the new layer of snow and ice. She stepped with care, aware of potholes and other dangers camouflaged by the white slush.

The air hung thick, nearly as frozen as the water in the harbor. Thankfully, the wind that swept out of the hills into the harbor died to a mere ruffling of the wool scarf wrapped loosely around her neck.

The winter sun dipped lower, a dim glow as

she reached the Fleet Administration building. A purpose-driven structure of gray concrete, crumbling at the corners. Whether intended or not, the squat ugly building blended perfectly with the ragged hills surrounding the harbor.

She stepped up the first of the three steps. The young sentry recognized her at once. He smiled and politely held the door open as she hurried inside.

Iranian Naval Base, Bandar-E Abbas

Iranian President Kaveh Mehran's fingers drummed at the top of the heavy table. Beads of perspiration glistened off his dark forehead despite the air-conditioned breeze that flowed silently around him.

The cool air picked up the aroma of fresh cut flowers neatly arranged in the middle of the table. The blooms were out of place in this drab, rundown room of Iranian Naval Headquarters. Aged paint that had once been some shade of white, now a dingy yellow, covered neglected crumbled sheet rock.

Under Mehran's feet, a threadbare rug lay tired and dull, bled of its once vibrant colors.

Except for the conference table and rickety brown office chairs, there was nothing. Windows thick with dust looked over a bare courtyard of sand and loose stone. A few hopeless weeds snaked along the ground. Like the rug, they lay dull and faded.

Mehran glanced at his watch. He fingered

the flowers, and tried not to locate the hidden cameras he knew were watching him. He was also sure microphones, everywhere, were listening. He hoped they could not hear his heart beat.

The Iranian president stroked the flowers. The smooth silken surface was cool and pleasant.

He jumped slightly as the door groaned open on tarnished brass hinges. A wave of warm sticky air flowed in scattering the aroma of the flowers.

Mehran wiped his sweaty palms on his pants.

Two senior clerics entered. Silent and pious, their simple earth tone robes flowed as if made of air. They moved one to each side of the door, and stood silent. The taller of the two looked around the room as if to inspect the condition. Satisfied, he nodded to someone unseen outside the door.

Supreme Leader Ayatollah Majeed Ali Sohrab entered. Except for his white beard, where his mouth was a thin, lipless slit turned down hard at the edges, the man who held real power over Iran, was a being of darkness.

His turban was an immaculate black as was his cloak and robes, with the sash around his thin frame in indigo silk.

Even darker were his eyes. Like black holes in space they seemed to capture all they saw. Even the light in the room seemed to dim as it flowed into those dark orbs.

"Peace be with you." President Mehran said as he bowed his head.

The taller of the clerics moved forward and pulled a chair from the rim of the table. Without looking, the Ayatollah lowered himself into the creaking chair.

"The news is good?" The Ayatollah asked. Without making eye contact, the old cleric lifted his arm, gesturing toward a chair.

President Kaveh Mehran took the seat offered. "Very good."

"Then tell me."

Mehran leaned forward. "The device works. The information was correct."

The Ayatollah seemed not to hear. "The source of this information, where is she?"

"Still serving at her post in Moscow."

The old cleric lifted a finger from under his robe. At once, the taller of the clerics was at his side. He leaned close to the old man's head. Words were whispered. The tall man nodded, then returned to his statue-like pose.

"What is your plan, Mehran?"

The President cleared his throat. "One of our submarines will carry out the mission. I invited you here so you could... bless its captain and crew."

The Ayatollah sat in a silence that throbbed with disapproval.

"Submarines, again." He muttered.

"It is the only way."

Sohrab bowed his head until it almost disappeared into the folds of his black robe. "I cannot be seen near it. I need only to know the date this operation begins and ends. When will you be ready?"

"A month," Mehran whispered.

At that the Ayatollah focused his black eyes on the President. "This time, you will not fail."

Mehran cleared his throat nervously. "I understand."

The old cleric straightened his back, "General Shatrevor was also your idea." His voice was quiet and cold. "Had the Zionists not been so concerned with the German submarine, that operation might have brought the world down on our heads."

"No one could have predicted that U-boat," Mehran answered.

"Your work is to foresee everything. This plan must be without fault. The time is right and Allah has blessed us with a weapon to eliminate the little Satan and his protector." Those black unblinking eyes pinned Mehran to his chair. "It is Allah himself who directs you."

The old cleric let the weight of his words sink in. "You fail because you do not hear His words and do His work. The Devil sends failure. Only an unbeliever allows Satan to stop such a vital task."

Mehran swallowed again. "It will not fail."

The Supreme Leader moved a gnarled hand in dismissal. "We will meet again, when it is time."

Lapadnaya Lista
Russian Submarine Base

What few hours of semi-daylight the Arctic winter allowed closed quickly behind her. The sky grew colder, as the faint glow of the sun died. A flurry of snowflakes announced another bleak night. She checked her watch as she hurried from the Fleet Administration Building. Every second counted.

USS CHURCHILL DDG-81
The Persian Gulf

"Man, that feels good," Lieutenant Jiminez announced as he stepped into the cool air of the destroyer's wardroom. "Bet I sweated off ten pounds up there today."

CHURCHILL's Weapons Officer rose from one of the faux leather covered sofas. "You guys kicked some serious butt up there today."

"All we needed was the word, and that boat would have been a nice new reef." Jiminez smiled as he peeled off his perspiration saturated flight suit.

"So, how are our shallow water tactics working?" The Weapons Officer asked.

Jiminez downed a glass of ice water, then filled it again. "Hard to tell."

The Weapon Boss's face wrinkled in confusion. "What do you mean? From what I saw, they worked great."

Jiminez drained another glass. "This guy was too easy. He didn't seem to understand in shallow water you have to think in three dimensions. Basically, he forgot to look up."

"Interesting." The Weapons Officer shrugged. "You'd think since the Russians trained these guys they'd know that."

"This one must have missed that day of class," Jiminez leered.

"Okay, write it up in your report. Might be useful."

The SEAHAWK pilot handed the now empty mug to the wardroom steward. "Will do, right after a nice cold shower."

Lapadnaya Lista
Russian Submarine Base

Warmth, more than light, glowed from the few bulbs that chased the dark and chill from the small apartment. In the air, the aroma of baked chicken, yams and yeast rolls wafted from the antique stove.

She glanced toward the desk. There lay the package, an official envelope properly marked, the seal fastened on the back. She smiled and giggled. It was time to make the tea.

Iranian Naval Base, Bandar-E Abbas

SIMCER's crew welcomed the night. The air cooled quickly as the sun sank into sea. Except for the hushed thrum of the KILO's diesels, the sea was silent. Three miles from the harbor, their escort waited. Tonight it was a low sleek boat, top heavy with guns and missile launchers.

The small submarine exchanged light signals with the escort, then dutifully fell in line astern. The gentle slap of waves along SIMCER's rubber-coated hull fell silent as the ships slowed.

Coded signals from the harbor watchtower to the escort granted permission to enter as both ships rounded the thin breakwater of rock and broken concrete. Ten minutes later, SIMCER made her lines fast to the dock.

The crew of the Iranian submarine went about their work quickly. Shore power cables snaked along the pier and connected to receptacles in the sides of the KILO's sail. The activity was fast but silent. Men rigged the submarine's topside so they could put their ship and themselves to bed.

Lapadnaya Lista
Russian Submarine Base

She hoped her face would not betray her, as she watched the door swing open.

Her husband, Valerik Danyankov, Commanding Officer of the AKULA Class submarine K-157 VEPR, stepped into the small entryway. Streams of frigid air followed him in.

He shut the door quickly as the wind groaned.

"Was today a good day?" She asked pleasantly as she helped with his heavy coat.

"No." He sighed, then turned and wearily smiled down at her.

"It could not have been *that* bad," Evelina Danyankov cooed. "Dinner is ready."

The VEPR's Commander lifted his nose. "Smells wonderful," he said as he pulled her to him. "Seems you are the only one I can count on these days."

"Now, Valerik," she said pulling away. "You should not be so down."

"I get more frustrated each day I have to deal with these cutbacks," he sighed again. "How can I keep my boat ready, when I get no support? Fleet Command refused me even three days at sea. Crew rations have been cut again. Advanced sonar training has been cancelled. Two more boats from Squadron Seven are on the list to be decommissioned. When will this end? How will it end?" He fumed.

Taking him by the hand, she led him toward the neatly set table. Halfway, she stopped.

"On the way back from the commissary, I stopped by Administration to check the housing list for two of new crew families." She stepped unconcerned around the desk. "They asked me to bring you this." She rested her finger on the brown-paper envelope. "Looks like you'll have another new crew member."

"What?" He snarled. "These were to go

directly to the ship." He stepped to the desk and glared down at the neatly wrapped package. "Lazy, that is what it is. My wife is not a messenger." He raised his finger, shaking it in the air. "I will fix them tomorrow. You just..."

"Valerik, stop, please," she said firmly. "Perhaps you should see who your new crewman is. I did not mind bringing it home."

Danyankov lowered his head. "You are right." He reached for her again. "After we eat."

"Should you not look at this new crewman first?"

"I just want to sit and relax."

"No," she responded. "You will be in a bad mood all night. Read it now, then we can eat and you'll forget all about it." She added a wink to her smile.

With a grunt, he picked up the package. "Must be a rating," he remarked as he felt the brown paper. "Not much in it." He turned it over, and tore open the cover.

"Look," he sneered. "Wrong folder for a rating, probably ran out of correct envelopes."

He opened the folder. "Why have they sent this now? This man does not arrive for another... six months." He kept reading. "Name: Danyankov. Danyankov?" He murmured.

He read on, "First name, unknown." How could this man not have a first name? He flipped the page to where a photograph of a new member of the crew should be. Instead of a picture, there was an image.

Danyankov's mind knew this type of image.

It was the same as a printout from VEPR's passive sonar. The image was confusing, but his eyes soon made out a tiny head, a torso, legs and an arm. On the border of the image was neatly typed letters that read, "Mother-Evelina Danyankov."

He felt a lightening bolt of understanding slam the front of his head. He suddenly felt hot. His legs trembled under him. It was hard to form words. He turned to his smiling wife.

"A b-baby?" He stammered.

"Yes," she giggled. "Our first baby." She put her arms around him. "You are trembling!"

For the first time in his life, he was unable to respond, unable to think. *What was this that filled him? Fear? No, he had known fear, and this was not it.* He did not understand what it was; he just knew that he had never felt more alive. Then warm tears rolled from his eyes.

"Are you happy?" She asked softly against his chest.

Danyankov closed his arms around her.

"Happy?" He suddenly laughed and picked her up. He spun her around nearly knocking the lamp from desk.

"I've never seen you like this," she said, taking his face in her hands.

"I've never felt like this," he responded. "Do we know?" He asked.

"Do we know what?"

"Boy or girl?"

She reached for the image. "Hm, look here." She pointed to a place on the image. "Looks like your little sailor has a periscope," she giggled.

Valerik Danyankov laughed again. "This has to be the best day of my life." He crowed.

"Come, now," she urged softly. "Dinner will get cold."

He rocked her in his arms, his chin in her sweet smelling hair. From somewhere deep in his mind, a sad yet wonderful thought surfaced. *Not far from here, my mother gave my father the same glad news.*

Chapter Three

JONAH

"Man is born to trouble,
as the sparks fly upward."
~Job 5:7

Iranian Naval Base, Bandar-E Abbas
Senior Officer's Quarters
December 20th

"I am awake." Commander Feroz growled at the knocking on his door.

For a moment, there was silence. "Sir, will you attend morning prayers?" The voice of the unseen crewman asked cautiously.

Feroz stepped to the door, and tore at the lock and knob. His powerful hand swung the door open in such a rush, the thin wood smashed into the wall. His wild eyes met those of the young midshipman sent to rouse him.

The boy's face twisted in terror as Feroz's

scarred face seemed to reach for him. He stumbled back, tangled in his own retreating feet. With a dull thud his back hit the wall.

"That will be all." A soft, yet firm voice called from the narrow hall.

Both Feroz and the midshipman turned to see Admiral Dareh step through the door.

"Carry on with your duties," Dareh said as he brushed dust from the young officer's jacket.

"Yes sir," the youngster stuttered. He stepped around the tall slender senior officer and bolted for safety.

Feroz shifted his eyes to the Admiral. "What do you want?" He rasped.

Dareh looked down. His aristocratic features a stark contrast to the shorter man's rough and damaged face.

"Such a ray of delight in a dull world." He murmured, smiling slightly.

Feroz stepped back into the room.

"From your report, yesterday's operation was less than successful." Dareh noted as he entered.

SIMCER's commander turned to face his guest. "Is that why you are here?"

"Partially." Dareh looked out the window. "Is there no way your submarine can evade the Americans?"

Feroz's eyes narrowed. "Why else are you here?"

Moscow, Russia

Irisa Rulyuk took her time going home today. The long-dreaded algebra test was over. She had done well, and the relief showed in her step as she walked slowly along Rubcovskaja Street with the cold crisp air nipping at her cheeks and nose.

No more studying, no more numbers and word problems. Tonight she could enjoy herself.

Uncle Gregor was coming for the holiday, and she smiled as she thought of her favorite uncle. He always had jokes and funny stories. He also brought toys and candy.

Of course, she would have to give up her bed to him, but it was worth it. She and her little sister would share a mattress under the dining table. They would listen to the adults talk, whispering and making each other giggle until they fell asleep.

After she crossed the irrigation canal off the Yauza River, Irisa turned right along a patch of neatly cultivated and tended woods known as Metallurg Park. The path eased gently along the edge of the narrow river. Great trees, now bare of leaves, lined the path. Icicles hung from branches where summer green had been. She liked how the ice made the park look as if it were made of glass.

Small streams snaked along cutting back and forth at the edge of the asphalt pathway. When the months were warm, her family picnicked here. The river and streams would gurgle and splash against the smooth rocks as their cool water swept toward the Moscow River. Now the water lay silent in frozen slush, barely moving.

She neared her favorite spot, a small bridge of rough-hewn wood. Here, she could watch sticks and leaves float in the black water as they made their way into the river. Often, she wondered where they went as they tumbled and floated along.

The thick rough timbers muffled her steps as she topped the bridge and looked over. The water was dark. Thick chunks of ice and slush flowed along in the slow current. Irisa's eyes followed a small twig as it floated from under the bridge. She traced its wake back to where it had emerged.

She gasped when she saw a hand poking up from the inky-black water. Not sure what she'd seen, she crossed the bridge and stepped down the steep bank. Careful of her footing, she looked under the bridge, and stumbled back into the slush as her eyes focused on the hand and the body it was attached to.

It was a woman. Her head and shoulders protruding just above the ice. In the fading light, Irisa could she had been a pretty woman not much younger than her own mother. She looked like a doll, with a blue face, as if the maker had yet to paint in the details.

The woman looked so beautiful, so peaceful. It reminded her of when she had seen her grandma's body. She had not been afraid then, and she was not afraid now.

Irisa peered further into the gloom under the bridge and saw another body. This one was a man. Fat and ugly. His face lay across the woman's hips. The side of his head was gone with a jagged hole just above his left eye. From his open mouth something red and frozen hung like sharp terrible teeth.

The spell of the beautiful woman broke, and Irisa's scream echoed through the woods in the cold Moscow evening.

Iranian Naval Base, Bandar-E Abbas

"You seem nervous?" Commander Feroz rasped as he and Admiral Dareh entered the heavily guarded building.

Dareh stopped and regarded him. "Mind yourself, Commander." He said softly, "You will be speaking with our President. To him you are merely a tool, one that can be replaced."

Feroz dry spat. "Politicians."

A team of President Mehran's security detail watched the approaching officers. One of them checked their badges and identification cards. Another pulled a couple of official photographs from a locked brief case and compared each man's face. No courtesies were exchanged as Dareh and Feroz passed through the layered security.

"Wait!" Ordered the detail team leader. He spoke into a hand-held radio.

Seconds later the heavy door of the Base

Commander's office door swung open. Another security guard went through, looked around, then motioned the two men forward.

As dictated by naval custom, Dareh entered first. When both were inside, the door closed silently until the steel lock clicked into place.

The room was airless with heavy linen shades drawn down over the windows. Only the bulb of a desk lamp lit the gloom where the President, his Minister of Defense and the Base Commander were waiting.

"Reporting as ordered." Dareh announced.

"Ah, Admiral," President Mehran said warmly as he stood beside the desk. He extended his hand.

Dareh stepped forward and took the Iranian President's hand. "It is an honor, sir." He said as he bowed his head in submission.

Mehran turned his eyes to Feroz. "And this is the submarine captain I have heard such good reports about?"

The Admiral stepped to the side. "Sir, may I present Commander Feroz, Commanding Officer of the submarine SIMCER?"

"You may indeed." Mehran smiled as he again extended his hand.

Feroz stepped forward into the lamp light to shake his hand.

President Mehran's thin lips, curled into their familiar fake smile, froze when he saw Feroz's face. The scar seemed on fire as the weak energy of the bulb amplified the ghastly wound. Mehran quickly regained his composure. "Captain, it is indeed a pleasure."

Feroz's thick powerful hand wrapped around Mehran's thin fingers. His eyes never left the President's.

"Well, then," Mehran said uncomfortably. "Let us talk." He pulled his hand from the vise-like grip of SIMCER's Commander and motioned him to sit.

Once Feroz was seated, President Mehran lifted his upturned palms to the ceiling and spoke fiercely.

"Brothers, Allah has blessed us at last with the ability to strike a great and fatal blow at our enemies." He paused, letting the words hang for a moment. "All that is needed is a means to carry Allah's wrath to their front door."

He let his arms slowly fall. "Commander Feroz," he said, his voice charged with zeal, "You have the honor of being Allah's messenger."

He let his hand rest on Feroz's shoulder. "Brothers, our scientists have discovered the means to destroy the very heart of the United States. Our target is not a person, not a building." He paused. "It is an entire city."

The effect the President sought was immediate as gasps hissed from the four men he had assembled.

"Brothers, I know the question your eyes ask." Now Mehran's lips curved into a deadly smile. "It is New York."

"How?" Feroz blurted out.

"That is to be discussed later," Mehran crooned. "What we need is a method of transporting your submarine into the heart of New York Harbor."

"But, Mr. President," Dareh said, nervously eyeing the Minister of Defense sitting behind the desk. "Our submarines are coastal craft."

Mehran's glared back at him. "You will find a way, Admiral."

"If only your submarines were made of oil." The Minister of Defense, a pale fellow in an immaculately pressed uniform, spoke for the first time. "Then the Americans would welcome you with open arms." He chuckled at his own humor.

Mehran expelled something like a laugh. "How true, Respected Minister. But there must be some way..."

"That is only one of our problems." The Minister of Defense continued. "What do you think will happen when American satellites find one of our submarines sniffing at their shore?"

Admiral Dareh shuddered. "It could be war, before our plan is ripe."

"Wait!" SIMCER's Commander got to his feet and rushed to the windows. He lifted the heavy shade from the center one.

The President's bodyguard by the door stepped forward, but Mehran waved him back. "Yes, Commander?"

Feroz stood motionless as he stared over the harbor and the naval repair yard.

"Commander!" Admiral Dareh demanded,

"What are you thinking?"

"That ship, tied up over there. What is it?" Feroz asked.

"An oil tanker, the *Behzad Nabavi*. Bound for Venezuela." The Base Commander responded in a choked voice. Unlike the Minister, he was an untidy man, hastily squeezed into his dress uniform.

"Why is she in the Navy Yard?" Feroz asked.

"A fire in her steering room. Could not maneuver so we towed her in for repairs."

"How long will those take?"

"You... I will have to check." The Base Commander stammered.

"She carries more than just crude, I assume?" Feroz growled.

The Minister of Defense's eyes slitted. "That is a state secret."

Feroz turned from the window. "Do we know when the American satellites pass over?"

"Of course!" The Minister's voice held both pride and curiosity.

"Where are you going with this, Commander?" Dareh hissed.

"Jonah." Feroz said quietly.

Dareh shook his head. "What?"

"I need control over the entire yard." Feroz almost vibrated with thought. "And I need that tanker."

"Captain Feroz!" The Base Commander leaped to his feet. "Why should I turn over..."

Now Feroz's eyes seemed to blaze. "I have no time for explanations."

The Base Commander turned to Admiral Dareh. "There is a chain of command!" He objected.

Dareh also stood. "Commander Feroz, you are not the admiral here."

President Mehran lifted a hand. "Silence."

When the room had quieted down, Mehran asked."You have a plan?"

Feroz crossed his arms. "Yes."

Mehran looked around at the assembled men. "Who else has an idea?"

No one spoke.

"As I thought." The President sighed. He turned to the Defense Minister. "You will give him what he needs."

"But, sir!" Dareh protested.

President Mehran cut him off. "As will you, Admiral, and you, Base Commander."

With no emotion, Feroz stepped to the door. "I must begin now."

Mehran smiled. "Of course, Commander." He nodded at the bodyguard who opened the door, and Feroz strode out.

Admiral Dareh took a deep breath. "Mr. President, I do apologize…"

"For what?" Mehran answered in a growl. "For having a man of ideas, when all of you sit here with dull minds?"

"But Feroz is…"

"What?" Mehran asked quietly. "A warrior? An instrument of Allah's work? Is that what you were going to say, Admiral?"

Dareh was silent.

"His face?" Mehran asked. "What happened to him?"

The Admiral looked up. "Commander Feroz was a young lieutenant on the Frigate SAHAND," he answered quietly.

President Mehran shrugged his shoulders. "Explain what you mean, Admiral."

"On April 18th, 1988, SAHAND was ordered into action against the American fleet. She cleared the harbor and fired on an American A-6 fighter-bomber. She missed, but the Americans did not. The frigate took hits from two HARPOON missiles. On the bridge, Feroz saw the first one was aimed directly for them and shoved his captain out of the way." Dareh took in a deep breath. "When the missile exploded, shrapnel tore his face apart."

Mehran shivered. "And how do you know this?"

Dareh bowed his head. "I was that captain. In saving me, he almost died for his trouble."

Mehran nodded, and said thoughtfully, "By the grace of Allah, he was not killed."

Admiral Dareh's eyes narrowed. "Part of him was."

Chapter Four

KEYS TO THE KINGDOM

*"The life of spies is to know,
not to be known."*
~George Herbert:
Outlandish Proverbs, 1640

Ministry of Defense
The Kremlin
Moscow, Russia
December 21st

Minister Zivon Vitenka looked over the endless stacks of paper that crowded his desk. Every concern of the Russian military had been his responsibility for so long now.

Though still early in the morning, he had already approved a new style of boots for paratroopers, authorized the manufacture of composite noses for MIG-29 fighters, and approved the list of movies to be supplied to strategic missile submarines.

He gathered the collar of the knit cardigan around his neck. Yet again the steam heat in his office had failed and a damp chill wrapped around him. He took up the steaming mug of strong tea from its trivet on his desk. The warmth of the ceramic penetrated his arthritic hands and soothed the stiffness that seemed to worsen each day.

He glanced out his triple pane one-way window. The thick snow that had started when he arrived before dawn had added to the drift already piled against the glass. He sipped at the sweet tea.

A shrill buzz on the office intercom interrupted his peaceful moment. The Russian Defense Minister snatched the phone from its cradle.

"Yes," he answered trying to hide his annoyance. He listened for only a second. "Send him in."

The door office opened before he had hung up the phone. Security Director Igor Minov walked briskly to the desk.

"Minister, we may have a problem," Minov started without the usual pleasantries.

Vitenka looked up at him. "Must it always be a problem with you?"

"Sorry, sir."

"Well, what is it now?" Vitenka asked as he drained the last of his tea.

"There was a double murder yesterday in Metallurg Park."

"I believe that is an affair for the police."

Minov opened the briefcase he always carried. "Yes, Minister, it is. It was the police that alerted Security Services."

Vitenka's brow wrinkled in confusion. "And why is that?"

"Because this man was murdered." The Security Director handed Vitenka a photograph.

Vitenka studied the picture a moment. "Who was he?"

"Vladimer Gorosi. The Chief Archivist in the classified documents department."

Vitenka peered closer at the photo. "I do not know this man."

"Not many did." Minov answered with a shrug. "For the most part, he stayed to himself."

Vitenka laid the picture on his desk. "You said a double murder."

Minov again reached in his briefcase and held up another photo. "He was found with this woman."

The Minister glanced at the new picture. "Nice looking. Who was she?"

Security Director Minov slid the photo back in the case. "We are not certain, but we have an idea." He now read from a note pad. "On her right hand, we found traces of gunpowder."

"A murder suicide?" Vitenka asked.

"It did not match the powder residue from the man's clothes or wounds. It appears she must have shot back."

Vitenka leaned an elbow on his desk. "Have you identified her?"

Minov frowned. "That is what worries me."

"Enlighten me, Director."

"Identification found in her coat pocket says she was a Mrs. Narkissa Kolchin."

"And?" Vitenka asked.

Minov took a deep breath. "Mrs. Kolchin was 82 when she died, eleven years ago." He paused. "When we add it all up, we may have the makings of a serious security breach."

"Anything else?" Vitenka asked quietly, looking down at the man's photo again.

"She was not Russian. We are checking, but she looks... Persian."

Vitenka got to his feet. "From Iran? That is troubling." He handed the photo back. "Have a team inventory those archives. Check into this dead archivist's secrets, and Director..."

"Yes, Minister?"

"Find out who that woman was!"

Nuclear Attack Submarine
USS TEXAS SSN 775
The Mid-Atlantic
December 22nd

She moved in desolate nothingness. Her perfectly designed hull flowed along as if she herself were made of seawater. Silence surrounded her. Even the usual noises of biologics: whales, shrimp, fish, were absent.

This part of the ocean was a desert of water.

Four-hundred feet above, wind-driven swells rose like writhing grey mountains. Some, as high as forty-feet, might have peaked higher except for the gale that tore off the tops. Now decapitated, the giant waves spewed geysers of white foam as they fell back into the angry sea.

The crew of TEXAS felt none of the winter storm raging above. Insulated in their steel cocoon, those aboard the newest American submarine serenely sailed east.

In the attack submarine's control room, there was silence. The Diving Officer had the ship in perfect trim, which left little work for the planes-men to keep her at the assigned depth.

At the Fire Control station, the watch tried to keep alert by conducting attack simulations on computer-generated enemy submarines.

In Sonar, the four-man watch team looked and listened to nothing, except for the storm above.

TEXAS had settled into her routine. The apprehension of deployment was over, and she was still ten days from her Persian Gulf patrol station. For most of her crew, this was their first deployment.

Thoughts of home, of women, and fears swirled through the new ship. The old hands wondered about the ship herself. What unseen flaw would rear up at the wrong time? Had the designers thought of everything? Could these young people be trusted when it mattered most? What was their mission?

Silently, the newest member of the Naval Submarine Force sailed toward the unknown.

Lapadnaya Lista
Russian Submarine Base

"Valerik, please," Evelina Danyankov pouted. "You will drive us both out of our minds. I am fine, so is the baby. Don't worry so much."

But..."

"Now go," she urged. "I have to get to the market."

The man known to the navies of America and Britain as The Prince of Darkness bowed his head. "Do you think I will be a good father?"

His wife gently placed her arms around his neck. To see him this way melted her heart. A man so tough, a man so feared, who feared no one. This man, this submariner who made life or death decisions. This man, who knew everything about ships, weapons and war, knew so little of himself.

"Of course you will," Evelina whispered in his ear. "You already are."

Iranian Naval Base, Bandar-E Abbas

Work on the tanker's fire damage halted. The relieved repair crew had no complaints since the temperature in the damaged compartment hovered around 120 degrees.

Commander Feroz walked along the tanker's 800-foot deck, a set of the ship's plans under his arm. He paced off approximate distances, made notes, and compared the plans to another set, those of SIMCER.

The shrill whistle of a tugboat ricocheted across the hot harbor air. Feroz checked his watch. *Thirty-five minutes until the next satellite pass.*

Feroz looked over the side. Five stories below, the tug waddled alongside the massive black hull of the *Behzad Nabavi*. Behind the tug, a barge eased into place next to the tanker. In the center of the rusted hunk of floating steel were seven massive pumps. Behind them was a stack, 20 feet high, of inch thick, high-tensile steel plates.

Feroz again checked his watch. *Twenty minutes..*

Once the barge was secured, Feroz waved his arm over his head. The *Behzad Nabavi's* forward crane grunted and squealed as the boom swung over the side.

Behind him the forward hatch cover inched open. Sunlight quickly filled the cavernous hold of the huge tanker, as the cover slid slowly on greased bearings.

The first three of the seven pumps were now swinging in the air over the hatch. With just enough room to clear, they descended to the bottom of the tanker's hull.

Feroz again checked the time. "Move!" He barked into his two-way radio.

Minutes later, three more pumps came over the side and down into the hull. The crane's cable creaked under the strain.

"Faster!" Feroz shouted again.

The last pump settled with a thud in the tanker's belly and Feroz checked his watch once more. "Fifteen minutes!" He roared into the radio.

The first six steel plates came up and over. The cable creaked louder under the weight.

"Add two more on the next lift." Feroz demanded.

"Sir, the cable..." A voice crackled back at him from the radio.

"Get those plates up!"

Two minutes later, eight plates moved up, swung over and were lowered. Feroz squinted at his watch face and rasped into his radio. "All the rest now!"

The massive tanker leaned slightly as the huge weight was now borne up by her hull. The crane's cable reel slipped and screeched as the wires that made up the cable neared the point of failure. At the crane's support base, 7 centimeter thick bolts vibrated as tonnes of pressure stretched the mounting holes.

Swinging its load over the gaping hold, the crane struggled. The electric motor powering the cable reel howled. The reek of ozone filled the hot air. The great load seemed to pause a moment, before the cable slowly lowered its burden.

As soon as the plates had disappeared

below, Feroz ordered the hatch shut. The massive cover rumbled as it moved to conceal their work.

Three meters from the old tanker's bottom, the cable could take no more. Strands of tortured wire snapped. With a cannon-like blast, the five centimeter wire rope parted above the hook.

Free of its load, the cable released built-up energy as it launched itself straight up. At over 600 kilometers an hour, it snaked in a blur out of the hatch, and arched 12 meters above the boom. Men dove for whatever cover the deck could offer as the cable lost its battle with gravity and began to fall. Like a giant enraged serpent, the wire whipped the air as it landed in a deadly coil of razor sharp steel shards.

Those on deck were fortunate. The rim of the hatch combing provided shelter from the shattered wire. The men working deep in the hold were less fortunate. For them, there was nowhere to go.

In the tanker's dark belly, a scene of horror unfolded as if in slow motion. The three meters the plates fell gave the steel the kinetic energy of a small bomb. As the plates dropped onto those already landed, air pressure had nowhere to go. Tonnes of force blew out and struck the men who were guiding the plates into position.

Knocked off their feet into the frame bays, they lay dazed and bleeding. As the pressure under the plates reached its peak the topmost plate slid forward until it tipped from the top of the stack and, like a blade, sliced through those now unable to move. The muffled booms of the impact drowned out their death screams.

As the hatch cover finally slid into place with a thump, Feroz checked his watch.

"Three minutes left!" He crowed.

Chapter Five

SINS OF THE FATHERS

"God has no power over the past
except to cover it with oblivion."
~Pliny the Elder

Ministry of Defense
The Kremlin
Moscow, Russia
December 22nd

"We found her!" Security Director Minov said eagerly as he came in the office.

Minister Vitenka looked up from signing a form. "And who was she?"

Minov handed him a folder. "Adara Binte Nawar. As I suspected, Iranian."

"An operative?" Vitenka asked.

"Mostly certainly. Internal Security has had her marked for the past six months, but considered her low priority. Been in Russia for five years and somehow stayed hidden until last spring."

Vitenka laid the folder on his desk. "Who killed her?"

Minov crossed his arms. "That we do not know. It would seem to be more than merely random."

Vitenka sat back in his chair. "And our archivist?"

"Minister, this has all the marks of a recruitment. Why else would such an attractive woman be with a man like him?"

"Yet he was married?"

Minov cleared his throat again, "Yes, sir. Three children, two girls and a boy."

Vitenka tapped his pen on the desk. "Does the wife know about this other woman?"

"We think not yet, Minister." Minov answered.

Vitenka turned to look out his window. "Then do not tell her."

Minov scowled. "But... he was a traitor!"

"Perhaps," Vitenka responded quietly. "But the wife was not."

Minov shrugged as his gaze fell to his boots. He slid his briefcase under an arm.

"Have the archives been examined?"
"Completely! Nothing caught my team's attention except... There was something strange..." Minov fiddled with the lock on his briefcase.

"What?" Vitenka asked, his attention only half on what his Security Director was saying.

"None of the most secret files were touched. We verified every original seal. None tampered with." Minov paused. "The only ones disturbed were from the early 1960s."

Vitenka turned back from the window, "When?"

Minov opened his briefcase and pulled his pad out.

"One entire folder is gone. But we found its cover, mis-filed. It was a project called..." He read from his pad. "MAY HARVEST."

Busy with his notes, the Director of Security failed to notice the blood drain from the Defense Minister's worn face.

Minov continued. "I am surprised such old information would still be classified." He rolled his shoulders. "And why would anyone kill for it?" He slid the pad back into his case, and looked up. "Minister?" Alarm in his voice. "Are you unwell?"

Vitenka's eyes were wide, with a distant stare. His hands, flat on the desktop, trembled as if with an ague.

"Minister?" Minov spoke louder.

Vitenka snapped out of his fit. "Security Director Minov," he hissed. "Find out every single person this woman contacted. If those files are still in Russia, they must be retrieved!"

Minov's face showed his confusion. "But sir, it is all ancient history. I do not see how...."

Vitenka cut him off. "You have no need to understand. Go and bring them back!"

When the door had clicked shut behind his

Security Director, Vitenka picked up his phone, punched a button and waited for the connection to be completed.

"I need to see the President immediately."

Russian AKULA Class
Nuclear Attack Submarine
K-157 VEPR

Nuclear Technician Boris Klitnyy knew how a condemned man felt. The scrapes on his knee and forehead stung, and only added to the young man's misery.

Lieutenant Shurgatov had offered some comfort, however, other members of VEPR's crew avoided him as if he were infected with some contagious disease.

Klitnyy busied himself as best he could. Secondary steam isolation valves deep in the AKULA submarine's hull needed maintenance. He took his small canvas tool pouch, checked his flashlight, and walked to the ladder that descended into the belly of the Russian submarine's propulsion plant.

Just as he was about to step down the first rung of the ladder, Shurgatov took him by the shoulder.

"Captain needs to see you." The young officer said solemnly.

Klitnyy looked into his Divisions Officer's eyes for hope, but found none. He stepped away from the ladder, set his tools down, and with head bowed began the walk forward.

He did not have far to go. The Lord and Master of VEPR, Captain First Rank Valerik Danyankov met him in the passageway.

Klitnyy shook as he stood before his commander.

"What happened, Boris?" Danyankov asked calmly.

Those within hearing twisted their heads. *Boris? Our Captain speaking to a man by his first name?*

Klitnyy's mouth went dry, but he quickly recovered. "Sir, I had just been to the calibration shop for compartment seven's radiation detectors. I did not see the ice on the casing. The detectors went over the side when I... fell." Klitnyy lowered his head as though ready for it to be lopped off.

"You have a family?" Danyankov asked softly.

"Yes, sir." Klitnyy whispered. "Two boys, and another on the way."

Danyankov turned to Shurgatov. "Have the Deck Officer get the ice cleared from the casing." VEPR's Commander put his hand on Klitnyy's shoulder. "It is good you did not go over the side, too." He smiled. "Has the Medic seen you?"

Those who could hear, thought they were in a dream. *What has happened? Where was our Captain?* This man looked like Danyankov, sounded exactly like him but what they had just witnessed was not the Captain they knew.

And it was not relief they felt. Surely it was the end of the world. The balance of power, the status-quo had suddenly shifted, and no one knew why.

They were used to the fear they felt for Captain First Rank Danyankov. It had become part of what VEPR was. *What had caused this change in their Commanding Officer?* A new fear swept through the ship like a sickness.

Office of Naval Intelligence
Washington, DC.
December 23rd

"This is not how it used to be." Commander Sills grumbled as she reached for the page the printer spat out.

Lieutenant Mark TO laughed, "You mean they don't write on stone tablets anymore?"

"No, Smart ass!" She shot back. "We used to have to dig and put pieces together. Real spy stuff." She paused as she read the paper. "Now the bad guys send press releases."

The Lieutenant turned from his computer screen. "What's going on?

"The Iranian Navy just announced a major exercise to celebrate the new year."

TO rolled his eyes. "Last time that happened, they got a little too close to one of our destroyers." He stretched his arms behind his neck. "That was a mess."

"Yeah, I remember," Sills said as she

continued to read. "Oh-oh, this is going to be interesting."

TO scooted his wheeled chair toward Commander Sills. "What now?"

"The boys are flexing their muscles. Planning a live fire exercise to test their new torpedo."

"A new torpedo?" asked TO. "They don't have anything new, do they?"

Sills shook her head. "Not that I know of."

TO returned to his computer. "Let me see who's in the area."

"Before you do that, take a look at the last satellite pass over Bandar-E Abbas."

TO nodded and tapped the request into his keyboard. A moment passed. TO squinted as an image filled the screen. "Nothing new. Three KILOs, a frigate. That damaged tanker's still there and four small boats. Not many people around." He shrugged. "Looks normal to me."

"Something's up," Sills growled. "These people don't fire off real torpedoes. Don't have enough as it is." She poked her pen into her chignon. "Like my Dad used to say, 'This don't smell right.'"

"Want to run this up the line?" TO asked.

"We better get our ducks in a row first. Who can do a little snooping?"

Again, TO tapped the keyboard. "Surface action group's operating with REAGAN, but that does us no good." TO used his mouse to scroll down a list of U.S. and friendly naval assets in the region. "HMS SCEPTER's in the

Indian Ocean," he announced. "Two days out."

Sills leaned back in her chair. "We have any boats in theater?"

Once more, TO tapped the keys. "TEXAS is due in on the 28th."

"Okay," Sills sighed. "Let's type it up real nice, and pass it along."

The Kremlin
Moscow, Russia

President Sergi Atopov shook his head, "This is madness, Zivon."

Minister of Defense Vitenka nodded.

Atopov rubbed his thin face. "You are sure it will work, after all this time?"

"I am positive."

Atopov looked down at the smooth surface of his desk, fury vibrating off him in silent waves. "Why was I not told of this before?"

Vitenka drew in some air. "No one since the Great Khrushchev has been told."

"Will the Iranians use it? Could they?" Atopov asked as if to find some hope.

"At the time, it was a simple matter. Development of a device would have taken three months." Vitenka sighed. "Now with computers, it could take mere days."

The President closed his eyes. "What about my first question?"

Vitenka met Atopov's eyes, "They will."

Chapter Six

ALL THE WORLD'S A STAGE

"Reality is merely an illusion,
albeit a very persistent one."
~Albert Einstein

Iranian Naval Base, Bandar-E Abbas
December 23rd

Crews of fifty men rotated every twelve hours. None of them knew what they built or why.

Conditions inside the tanker's massive hold were just short of hell. The temperature rose to 135 degrees. In areas where the welders worked, it went higher.

Captain Feroz allowed four blowers to be rigged. These drew air from the shaded area of *Behzad Nabavi's* foc'sle into the steaming hold. They did little to cool the cavern of steel, but at least the air moved.

After three day's work, the giant box

proceeded to Feroz's satisfaction. Once cut to fit inside the tanker's rounded bottom, the plates hung from electric hoists 90 feet above, until secured in place.

Torches flashed and sputtered as holes for the pump suctions were cut into the newly erected bulkheads. Workers not setting the forward and rear plates, fabricated walls. Others manufactured staircases, a small bunk room for twenty men, and a control station to operate the pumps.

On the fourth day, Feroz left the tanker for the first time. He always traveled after dark. Some thought it was because of the scar, others thought it best suited his nature.

He walked the half mile to an area few visited. To a civilian it was a junk yard; to the navy, it was a used surplus center.

For hours, Feroz walked among the rusting carcasses until he found what he needed.

A large cylinder tapered at both ends. The mass of rust, filled with stagnant foul water, had once been a boiler from a large ship.

SIMCER's Commander eyed it carefully. Its ten-meter length and four-meter diameter would do nicely.

Feroz moved aside as a crane, nearly as rusted as the old boiler, lumbered to a stop. Gears that had not known grease in years screeched as the boom hovered over the eight ton hunk of rust.

USS MIAMI SSN 755
NAVAL SUBMARINE BASE
Groton, Connecticut
December 24th

Commander Grant McKinnon dreaded the days ahead. It seemed to come faster each year and here it was again, another holiday with nothing but a big empty house and memories. He'd thought of getting a tree this year, but decided against it. Why make it worse?

MIAMI, like her Captain, was now a lonely ship. Half her crew had taken leave. The usual sounds of repairs and maintenance were absent, replaced by a peaceful, yet eerie silence.

McKinnon checked his wristwatch with a sigh. He knew he would have to go home soon, although he wished he could stay. He thought of visiting the cemetery, but dark came far too early at this time of year.

He picked up the last of the paperwork from his small desk. One folder marked TOP SECRET remained for him to review. He opened it and began reading.

Recent Encounters With Iranian KILO Class Submarines. McKinnon read the two-page document, making mental notes.

MIAMI would not deploy to the Gulf for another year, however, information was life and death for a submariner. Then he read about the helicopter's encounter with the submarine.

"Forgot to look up." He chuckled to himself.

Russian Submarine Base
Lapadnaya Lista

Valerik Danyankov could not help but watch Evelina. Everyday she seemed more beautiful. By the light over the sink, she was drying the last of the dinner dishes and putting them in the cupboard.

She caught his stare. "What is it?" she smiled, spreading the dish towel to dry.

"Nothing," he gave a grin. "Come sit."

When she'd snuggled beside him on the worn sofa, he placed his arm around her. "There is one thing we have not discussed."

"And what is that?" Evelina murmured.

"When do we tell the Grandfather?"

She was silent a moment. "I would like to wait on that."

Danyankov's smile faltered. "Why? Are you... all right?"

"Oh, I am fine," she smiled. "It is just that with my father, timing is everything. I want... to tell him in a way he will never forget."

"Ah," Danyanko smothered a yawn.

Then the smile fell away from her face as she searched his face. "Will you be here when the baby comes?"

"Of course," he cooed as he stroked her hair. "Where else would I be?"

"At sea somewhere. On a great adventure to

save the world."

"No," Danyankov sighed. "With the way things are, I think my adventures are over."

United States Naval Submarine Base Groton, Connecticut

It was only four when Grant McKinnon drove out the main gate. The sun had given up, allowing the dark gray to attend to what was left of the day. The air was perfect for Christmas Eve, with fat snowflakes gently falling in a steady curtain of white.

MIAMI's Captain wanted to avoid the lights and fuss of Groton on this night. He decided to take the back road home and set the four wheel drive. Danny had always loved the Kings Highway. He'd laugh as the car swooped over the rolling hills, around the corners and down the valleys. McKinnon smiled as memories flooded back, and could almost hear his dead son's giggles echoing from the back seat.

Little traffic had been along here since the snow started. Just a single set of tire tracks on the pavement through the thin, slippery blanket.

He noticed the few homes to each side of this stretch of two lane highway were dark and lifeless. He wondered if the owners were off somewhere warm for the season.

McKinnon slowed as he came to the Dead Man's curve. Only a quarter mile more to the

turn that would take him down the hill into
Mystic. Then he saw the tire tracks veer, the
rear set fishtail, and both go off the road. His
eyes followed the tracks into the snow, and
suddenly his heart thumped hard in his chest.

Taillights were glowing from an angle where
they should not. The car was in the ditch, its
nose crunched into a stone wall.

McKinnon gently touched the brake pedal.
His small SUV slithered to the side as the tires
sought traction. Skillfully, he steered onto the
shoulder of the curve.

His mind on fire, blood flowing hot he threw
the seatbelt off. In seconds he was out and
running back toward those glowing red lights.
He slipped once, caught his balance, tramped
on over the snow-covered weeds, and down the
slight embankment.

The car was a two-door blue rental.
Obviously so because it was not yet coated with
salt stains down its sides, as was every other
local vehicle, including his own

There was no movement from inside as
McKinnon wiped away the film of ice and snow
on the passenger side window. As he placed his
face close to the cold glass he was dreading
what he might see. Lumps of white covered the
interior. He breathed again, the airbags had
worked.

He squeezed his eyes and saw a figure over
on the driver's side silhouetted in the luminous
green dash lights. Then there was movement as
a hand and fingers jabbed at what could only

be a cell phone.

McKinnon tapped on the frosting glass. The figure jerked in the seat as if startled.

He pulled at the handle and the door screeched open six inches before getting wedged by the bowling ball sized rocks that lined the shallow ditch.

"Are you all right?" he called into the dark interior.

"I think so." A breathless voice answered.

McKinnon was surprised at how calm the voice was. He also noticed it was female. "That's good." Was all he could think to say.

"We can't get out. Both doors are stuck."

McKinnon reached down and felt for the obstruction. Thankfully, the ground had not yet to frozen solid. He found the edge of the large rock and worked his fingers under. Now he had more advantage, and with a grunt he flipped the rock over. It rolled down into the frozen trickle of the culvert. The smaller rocks came out with less effort. He wiped his hands on his black jacket and again pulled at the door.

The metal complained with a dull screech, although this time it swung wide.

"Come on," McKinnon urged.

"Take my daughter first," the voice called back. "Go on, Misty, this man will help us."

A tiny pair of hands reached out to him. As Grant McKinnon took hold of them, the feel of those tender hands sent a warm flood through him. It was something he had not felt since he last held his son. He reached under her arms, careful that her pink winter coat with faux fur at the cuff did not catch on the door.

"It's okay, I have you," he said softly as he eased her from the car, lifted her up to the side of the highway and set her on her feet in the falling snow.

"Mommy really did it this time," she said as she flipped her coat hood over her head.

McKinnon bent to look at her face in the dim light. Her curly auburn hair framed her face and her blue eyes were full of life, yet there was a sadness there.

"She sure did," McKinnon grinned. "Wait here while I get your mommy out."

"Got nowhere else to go," she said, looking around.

"How old are you?" Grant McKinnon chuckled.

"I'm four," she sighed.

"I'll be back," McKinnon smiled as he returned to the wrecked sedan.

Once again, at the open door, he reached in. "Can you make it?" he asked.

As the figure crawled across the passenger seat, McKinnon could see little of her in the dim interior. A slender gloved hand reached out. Grant took it and pulled gently. A head covered in the hood of a heavy winter coat emerged. McKinnon held her hand until she was out of the car and on her feet. Taking her arm, MIAMI's Captain led her up to the road.

"Thank you so much," she said as she stepped onto the flat pavement. "I turned off

I-95 to get gas and somehow wound up on this road," she explained. "We were looking for a place to turn around when I skidded."

"It happens," McKinnon smiled. "At least you're both okay."

"I don't know what we would have done if you hadn't come along," she said as she pushed the hood from her head.

Again, Grant McKinnon felt his heart thump. Her red hair flowed from under the rabbit fur-lined hood. It seemed to radiate fire even in the gloom of the snowy dusk. Her eyes were soft, yet wise. Her nose, well-shaped, blended perfectly into the smooth skin of her face. Faint patches of freckles accented the dimples along her cheeks.

"I'm happy to help," McKinnon stuttered, "Are you sure you're okay? Those airbags can be brutal."

"My face is a bit sore." She replied, pressing her gloved hands to her cheekbones.

The little girl stepped over the snow and reached for her mother's hand. "What do we do now?" She asked.

"It'll be okay, Pet," her mother answered.

"Is there anyone I can call for you?" McKinnon asked. "Your husband or…"

"There's no husband," she cut him off, turning her head to the crashed rental.

Grant McKinnon tried not to smile. Something he thought had died with his own family, stirred. "I know the Constable in this area. I can call in the report for you."

"How about a tow truck?" She asked, bringing her eyes back to his.

He shook his head. "No way we'll get one out here tonight."

"Hotels?" She asked.

"Doubt it. It is Christmas Eve."

"Mommy, how will Santa know where I am?" The girl asked.

She picked her daughter up and pressed her lips to the girl's cold reddened cheek. "He'll find you. I promise."

That something Grant McKinnon thought had died inside him, now took over. Without even thinking, his mouth opened. "You could stay with me." *You idiot!*

The little girl's face lit up. "Does Santa know where you live?"

"He sure does," McKinnon laughed.

"No!"The woman protested. "We couldn't impose on your family on Christmas Eve."

"There's no family," he replied in the same tone she'd said about there being no husband.

"Well, I mean... I don't even know you."

"Let me introduce myself then," he smiled. "I'm Grant McKinnon. I command a submarine stationed here."

"A sailor, huh?" She asked cautiously.

"Like a pirate?" The little girl asked.

For a second time McKinnon laughed, "Some people think so."

"Wait," the woman smiled. "Are you *the* Grant McKinnon? I thought you looked familiar. You were on the news last month, and all those talk shows."

McKinnon rolled his eyes. "Yup, that's me."

"Well, of all things!" She said as she slipped off her glove and extended her hand. "I'm Jennifer Dalton." She smiled as she placed her hand into Grant's, "And this is Misty."

"We've met," Misty said with a yawn. "Mommy, I'm cold."

McKinnon and Jennifer suddenly realized their hands were still together. Grant let go first. "Looks like you have to come now," he grinned. "Santa's not too far off."

Jennifer's nose wrinkled up. "That's not fair," she smiled.

"That is what we, in the submarine business call a sneak attack."

She looked again at the wrecked car, then down to her daughter. "Okay," she sighed. "I need to get Misty's car seat and our bags."

"I'll take care of that," McKinnon laughed with pleasure. It seemed to him he'd suddenly found a cache of laughter he'd not used in years. Not since...

"I have some... items in the trunk," Jennifer leaned toward him and gave a wink. "Wouldn't want Santa to miss your house."

Five minutes later, Misty was strapped into McKinnon's car, and the contents of the rental's trunk were safely stowed in the rear.

He opened the passenger door for Jennifer.

"Wow, an officer and a gentleman."

McKinnon closed the door quickly and hoped she hadn't seen him blush.

He drove off into the snow.

"Hey," the small voice called from the back, "Do you have a Christmas tree?"

McKinnon thought fast. "Not yet. Had to wait on someone to put the star on top."

"Me?" she asked.

"Of course," Grant answered.

Just before the village shops of Mystic, McKinnon slowed and turned into what had once been a gas station. Two men, each in flannel coats and matching hunting hats stood around a burning barrel of flaming pine branches. Around them, six or seven snow-covered trees stood waiting for last minute shoppers.

"Misty," he said as he opened the door. "You think you can help me find a nice one?"

"I sure can," she smiled back. "I'm a good tree picker."

Ten minutes later, Misty settled on a fine, full spruce. With thin nylon rope, the men strapped it to the roof of the car. Grant handed the older of the two the money.

He smiled at McKinnon, "Hope your nice family has a Merry Christmas."

Grant McKinnon felt every nerve in his body tingle. He tried to hide his smile, but couldn't. "We sure will. You and yours , too."

As they drove away, the snow grew thicker and heavier. Night had finally taken hold. Another half mile went by.

"Oh no," McKinnon said suddenly.

"What?" Jennifer asked.

"I almost forgot."

Jennifer looked puzzled. "Forgot what?"

"My Christmas cocoa."

"Cocoa?" Misty asked excitedly.

"Of course," McKinnon answered. "I think it's a law around here." He looked a question at Jennifer. She grinned and nodded.

McKinnon pulled off into the parking lot of the Seafarer Haven restaurant.

Misty's smile lit the darkness as McKinnon removed her from the car seat.

The young girl looked around. Lights twinkled from wreathes hanging on the lampposts. Through the windows of the stately Mystic homes, decorated trees glowed brightly, as did candles in upper floors.

"Wow," she sighed. "Mommy, it looks like the card Granny Ruth sent."

Jennifer seemed in awe herself. "Beautiful," she murmured as she took Misty's hand.

"Come on, we better hurry," Grant urged. "Don't want to miss out on the cocoa."

The three climbed up the steps, stomped the snow off their feet and opened the heavy wooden door to the antique restaurant. A tinkle of bells filled the air, and the scent of pine filled their noses.

Misty and Jennifer stood drinking in the festive view of a huge fire crackling in the stone hearth. Garlands hung in charming rows around the cream-colored walls. A tree festooned with what must have been miles of gold ribbon glimmered with just the right amount of tiny white lights. Real gaslights flickered warm and friendly on every round ornate table. In the center, glowed a great chandelier of brass arms accented with crystal globes. The lights from the tree reflected off the polished brass sending a shower of sparkles around the room.

Laughter rose and fell from the other diners, as the three of them stepped forward.

McKinnon got his first clear look at Jennifer, and was as transfixed by her beauty as she was by the decorations in this ancient eatery. For a while, both simply stared.

"Hey, you two!" Misty said, tugging on her mother's coat. "Are we going to get some chocolate?"

The adults snapped out of their stupor.

"Ah, sure," McKinnon smiled. "Let me take your coats."

A cheerful young hostess, complete with elf hat, led them to an empty table with a candle glowing in the center, and they settled down to read the menus.

McKinnon ordered the smoked seafood platter. Jennifer selected the clam chowder, and garden salad. After some debate and a few changes, Misty settled for fish nuggets with macaroni and cheese, as long as the cheese did not have any burned places on it, and of course, hot chocolate.

McKinnon struggled with what to say, what to ask. His mind burned with a thousand questions. He just did not know where to begin.

So start simple, he told himself. *Where are you from? What do you do?* He was just about to open his mouth when a booming voice ricocheted off the walls.

"Captain McKinnon!" The voice called, followed by a deep hearty chuckle.

McKinnon turned his head to see his Commanding Officer striding toward them.

"Hello, Admiral," McKinnon said as he got to his feet.

"Good to see you out tonight," Burke Tarrent smiled. He looked at Jennifer and Misty, then cocked his head toward McKinnon. His eyes spoke volumes. "And who have we here?" He asked with a broad grin.

"Uh," McKinnon stammered. "Jennifer Dalton, this is Admiral Burke Tarrent, Commanding Officer of Submarine Group Six."

"Submarine group?" Jennifer asked.

Tarrent chuckled. "In English, ma'am, that means I'm his boss."

"It's a pleasure meeting you," Jennifer smiled.

"And who is this pretty little lady?" Tarrent asked in a tone McKinnon would never have dreamed could come from his Commanding Officer.

Misty looked up at the Admiral. Her eyes took in his dress jacket and all the ribbons on his chest.

"I'm Misty," she answered. "Are you a pirate too?"

"Some people think so," Tarrent answered.

"You all say that," Misty responded as she took a sip from her cocoa.

"Well, Little Misty, it's very nice to meet you." The Admiral boomed.

A tiny line of whipped cream on her upper lip accented her smile. "Thank you."

"I'd better get back to my table," Tarrent said quietly. "Hope you have a Merry Christmas." The Admiral extended his hand to McKinnon. "Commander," he said with a sly smile. "Guess you'll need to drop by the office after the Holiday."

"Is that an order?" McKinnon asked.

"You betcha!" The Admiral gave a huge laugh and left.

Soon the chatter from the rest of the room died down as parties broke up, and the lights dimmed to a mere glow.

McKinnon and Jennifer's dinner talk was light and exploratory. No question probed too deep. No answer revealed too much. Misty sat quietly for the most part as she slurped the last of her chocolate. The fish nuggets and macaroni remained totally ignored.

"We just packed up and left," Jennifer explained quietly. "I want Misty to know me, know who I am." Her eyes became wet. "I was working so much I wouldn't see her for days."

Then she rubbed her eyes. "One day she gave me a picture she'd drawn. Told me it was of her so I wouldn't forget what she looked like." Jennifer took a long sip from her water glass. "So I sold the company three days later, the house a week after that, and here we are."

"Where were you going?" McKinnon asked.

Jennifer shook here head. "No idea."

Grant McKinnon was in uncharted waters and could not think of a thing to say, but felt he had to say something. "Well, I'm sure glad you're here."

Jennifer dabbed her eyes. "Me too."

With dinner done, the three made their way out into the chilly night. Fifteen minutes later, they pulled into the drive of McKinnon's house.

"Wow, this is really something," Jennifer gaped at the old Victorian house looming out of the falling snow.

"Built in 1867," McKinnon explained. "Its first owner was the Captain of a New London whaler."

"Beautiful," she whispered.

"Can we build a snowman?" Misty asked as she trudged through the ankle deep snow.

"Maybe tomorrow, Pet." Jennifer answered. "Now we need to see about getting you to bed. Remember, Santa will be here soon."

McKinnon fumbled with his keys until his fingers finally found the right one. The warm glow of the hall light greeted them as he swung the door open. He reached inside and flipped the switch for the main living room lights.

"Wow!" Misty said as she stood on the polished hardwood floor, and looked around at the antique furniture. Her eyes wandered over the walls lined with old paintings of ships and seamen, captains and pirates. "This place is like a moozeum."

"You mean museum," Jennifer giggled.

"That's what I said." The girl yawned.

Grant McKinnon brought in their bags and showed them their rooms. Leaving them to unpack, he retrieved the other items from the car. With the tree inside, the scent of the fresh cut spruce seemed as if it belonged. The aroma filled in the empty places in the house ... and in him.

Down in the basement, he dusted off boxes of Christmas decorations. Three hours ago, he would never have dreamed he'd be doing this.

A sliver of guilt slid into his heart. He was almost glad to feel it. Another emotion though dulled the ache, and Grant McKinnon caught himself whistling a Christmas carol.

Chapter Seven

THE LIST

"People are trapped in history,
and history is trapped in them."
~James Baldwin, Notes of a Native Son

Prison 44
Sirjan, Iran
December 25th

No one ever thought there was a need to pave the rutted path that wound its way through the foothills of the Zagros Mountains.

Even in the air-conditioned interior of the staff car, brown dust found a way in. The gritty powder clung in a film to all it touched. Metal, plastic, flesh, all became coated. It was as if the desert were rushing to claim any and all that ventured in.

Asha Feroz wiped the dust from his face. On this trip he had substituted his uniform for the only civilian clothes he owned. Tan shirt and brown slacks made of some synthetic material, and battered cloth slip-on shoes.

During the 160-mile trip from the Naval Base, Feroz had not said a word. The driver, a stout Military Security Officer, who knew the road well also knew just enough about his passenger to keep his own mouth shut.

It was early afternoon when he drew the car to a stop outside the main perimeter fence of 30-foot electrified chain link and razor wire.

Two sentries whose black uniforms the driver had never seen before, guarded a narrow rolling gate. As the driver lowered his window to present his papers, the gate rolled aside and one of the guards waved him through with no check of identification.

He nudged the car along a rutted path of packed dirt and sand. The hills grew taller as they wound their way closer. At the peak of a high rise, the road tapered off to a flat plateau surrounded by another fence constructed of steel poles steeply angled so as to make it impossible for a man to gain any type of hold. At the apex of the poles, more razor wire.

Within the fence, an unpainted blockhouse made of the same local rock, squatted on the dirt. At each end of its 20-foot high walls, square towers reared up, accented with searchlights and machine gun emplacements.

As at the first gate, Feroz's car passed through an electronic gate unchecked. At a gate of wrought iron, he finally stopped.

Two officers in the same strange uniforms as the sentries stepped out from behind the heavy iron gate.

The driver turned his head at the sound of the rear door snapping shut. His passenger had exited the car in a swift fluid motion.

The driver's brow wrinkled in confusion. He had been in the military long enough to know how strange it was that these officers rendered no salutes, and very few words.

He felt the bottom of his stomach drop as the passenger turned his head toward him, and that disgusting scar flamed in the afternoon sun. A breath of hot wind lifted his hair where it flared like a black halo for a second before settling back on his head. The eyes that were focused on him were lifeless and deep. He nodded slightly toward the driver.

"Feed him," he rasped to the black clad officers. Then they disappeared inside the gate.

Lapadnaya Lista
Russian Submarine Base

Evelina could not wait. Valerik had just enough time to plug in the old Christmas lights on the tiny tree before she shoved a neatly wrapped box into his hands.

"What is this?" He asked as he gently shook the box.

"Open it!" She giggled impatiently.

"No," Danyankov smiled. "Not till you open

one."

"Valerik, please."

Danyankov smirked, rolled his eyes, and tore at the paper.

Evelina, eyes wide, covered her mouth as her husband broked the tape that held the box together.

Danyankov opened the flap of cardboard. His smile faded. He dropped the box but held its content in his now trembling hand.

It was a simple black and white photograph, printed on poor quality paper. It was an old photograph, though newly framed and matted.

"My father and me," Danyankov whispered. He looked down at the proud officer holding his young son as he smiled for the camera.

"Yes," Evelina glowed. "I think it was taken on the first submarine he commanded. Look," she said pointing to the date neatly handwritten in the corner. "K-14 and my Sailors, November 1962. That was it, right?"

"It was," Danyankov answered as he ran his thumb gently over the glass. "That is my mother's writing."

"Do you like it?" Evelina asked.

The man in the picture looked so young, so happy, and proud. Danyankov's mind flooded with memories. Some of happy homecomings, others of sadness as he watched his father's submarine slip out to sea. He remembered nights when he could not sleep, as he wondered where his father was. What his father was doing. If he was safe. Had the sea monsters swallow ed him and the K-14?

"Valerik?"

Her voice floated to him and tugged him back.

"What?" He asked gently.

"Do you like it?"

"It is wonderful," he assured his wife as he reached for her. "Thank you."

"You still miss him, don't you?" she patted his cheek.

"Not as much as I should," he sighed. Then he broke away from her. "Now, it is your turn." VEPR's Captain got to his feet and walked to the tree. "Um, let's see," he teased.

"You are not good at this," she giggled.

Danyankov reached behind the tree and brought out a small rather crushed envelope. "Here it is," he said as he handed her the gift.

Her delicate fingers found another envelope inside the first. "What is this?"

"Go on," Danyankov urged.

She opened the flap cautiously. A single sheet of paper lay neatly folded inside. She slid the page out, and unfolded the paper, her eyes eagerly reading the lines.

From: Captain First Rank Valerik Danyankov (Commander K-157)
To: Admiral Vassili Vargin (Commander Northern Fleet)
Subject: REQUEST FOR TRANSFER
I do hereby request transfer from present command, Northern Fleet, Submarine Squadron

Seven, Combat Unit K-157 VEPR, to Northern Fleet
Advanced Training Command.
 I have completed 14 years and seven months of
at sea time.
Respectfully, Valerik Danyankov

Evelina's pretty lips made an O. She read
the letter again. "Why?" She whispered.

"It is time." He rolled his shoulders,
suddenly confused. "Does this please you?"

Evelina's head slowly bowed over the letter
she held against her chest. "I do not know."

"I thought... is this not what you wanted?"
He tenderly asked.

When she looked up at him, her eyes were
wet. "But your ship is so important to you. I
can not take that away from you."

He caressed her cheek, then lifted her chin.
"It is you that is important," he whispered,
kissing her lips quickly, adding as he cupped
his other hand over her belly. "And so is he."

Prison 44
Sirjan, Iran

Feroz seated himself at the dusty metal table.
The buff colored walls of the bleak room were
as lifeless as the rest of the prison. A single
bulb encased in wire and mounted in the
ceiling provided a yellow pool of light that fell in
the center of the table.

There was no sound, and no voices. Even
the air seemed muted as it hung hot and

heavy. No one would have known that more than a thousand men lived here.

The door behind SIMCER's commander opened. One of the black clad officers entered, carrying a stack of folders. "Here they are, sir," he said as he placed the folders on the table. "These match your request."

"Get to it," Feroz rasped.

The officer opened the first folder. "Name..."

"I need no names," Feroz hissed.

"Very well," the officer answered. "Prisoner 0198324, age 24. Five feet, nine..."

"Crime?" Feroz barked as he glanced at the man's photo.

The officer flipped to another page. "Arms theft."

"Family?"

"None."

"He will do," Feroz, answered. "Next."

"Prisoner 01987638, age 31. Height..." The officer caught the Commander's impatient gesture and continued, "Convicted of assault on a member of the Savama. No family."

"Any scars or tattoos?"

"None."

"He will do."

Two hours later, the stack had been gone through and Feroz's list complete: five numbers, five men.

Feroz stood. "I will have uniforms sent in four days. You will receive instructions as to how and when they are to be delivered. Do you understand?"

"Of course, Commander," the officer answered. "May I ask what the purpose of this team is? Perhaps I can suggest.." He stopped as the Commander froze as if preparing to lunge.

"You may ask," Feroz hissed. "And after I tell you, add your name to that list."

Chapter Eight

MOVEMENT

"I am become death,
the destroyer of worlds."
~J. Robert Oppenheimer

USS MIAMI SSN 755
December 27th

With little more than a swishing sound, the submarine's round form slipped effortlessly down the Thames River. The ice had retreated, leaving a narrow path into Long Island Sound and the Atlantic beyond.

Bundled and uncomfortable in his thickly padded exposure suit, Commander Grant McKinnon stood atop MIAMI's black, box-shaped sail.

Although he trusted his officers, he was relieved when the mouth of the river opened and the squat form of the Block Island lighthouse came into view through the mist.

Just short of the lighthouse, MIAMI slowed to allow the harbor pilot to climb off on to the waiting tug.

Free of the pilot and the river, MIAMI pushed forward again. Soon the water lifted over her bow and plunged down her sides in a graceful wave.

With his ship now safely in open water, McKinnon had no real purpose on the bridge. He looked blankly out into the cold afternoon. The gray-green water of the open sea stretched ahead, as the land behind sank out of view. *This is the best place for me*, he thought as the icy wind wiped at his exposure suit.

As suddenly as they had come, Jennifer and Misty were gone. Christmas had been wonderful. The old house had needed to hear the laughter of a child again.

Jennifer had promised to call when she got to wherever she was going, but McKinnon knew the chances of that were slim. Still, he was grateful for the time they'd had together. Now, thankfully he could occupy his mind with what he knew best.

It was only a short two days at sea. MIAMI's assignment was to play the role of bad submarine to a squadron of P-3 aircraft.

McKinnon would operate in shallow water 120 miles off New York. MIAMI would hide, and then give clues to her location, run and hide again. It would be a bit of a bore, but the sea time would clear the cobwebs out of his crew.

He hoped it would clear out a few of his own.

The Kremlin
Moscow, Russia

"What do we know?" Minister Vitenka asked in a whisper.

Security Director Minov ran his hand through his gray hair. "Very little," he sighed. "We have no indications of unusual activity."

"Perhaps that fact has something in it," Vitenka observed.

"I do not understand?" Minov responded as he crossed his legs.

"What is going on there? Is the lack of activity normal?"

"One of our naval analysts noted some grumbling among the yard workers," Minov noted with a shrug.

Vitenka sat up straight in his chair. "What kind of grumbling?"

"A sudden lack of manpower mostly," Minov explained. "From what our source says, fifty men and thirteen riggers vanished."

Vitenka's eyes narrowed. "These fifty men, what were their jobs?"

Minov reached into his briefcase. He flipped open a file tracing his finger down until he found the needed information. "I am not familiar with naval terms, but this says ship fitters and welders."

Vitenka was silent. He stared into nothing.

"Minister," Minov prompted him. "You seem to either know more about this than you care to tell on or have an idea."

Vitenka looked up. "That is true."

"Sir?"

"You have no knowledge of naval terms or anything naval. I need someone who does. Someone who knows what to look for."

"I am doing my best," Minov protested.

"I know you are, Director," Vitenka reassured him. "Your services have been exemplary. However, you have no background in naval affairs. I need someone who has. You will remain on this case but subordinate to Admiral Onufriev."

"I understand, sir."

"Meet with Onufriev within the hour. Brief him and get his input. I want you both back here by noon."

Iranian Naval Base, Bandar-E Abbas

Seven specially trained divers of the 3rd Iranian Commandos remained hidden in the cramped spaces of the tugboat's hull. Although night covered the scene, Feroz would not and could not take any chances. In tow fifty meters behind the tug, a rusted barge filled with scrap and other debris sluggishly followed.

Unseen, the real cargo hung under the junk barge. The old boiler, now sealed and weighed with 40 lead-filled barrels, strained at the cables that held it fast against the bottom of the barge.

Four miles from the base, Feroz pushed a button. On the barge hydraulic jaws closed on the cables. Tungsten blades set in the jaws sliced with ease through the straining cables. With only the splash of the severed wires, the boiler fell away from the barge and sank. As it settled into the sand and silt 150 feet below on the harbor floor, the commando team went over the side of the tug.

Using retarded lens lanterns, the divers quickly found the old boiler and went to work.

On the left side of the boiler, welders had installed a set of circular clamps. Two divers worked to open the clamps, while four others carefully guided a five-foot stainless steel cylinder into the clamps. Gently, the clamps shut around the cylinder. The divers tightened the holding bolts, then ascended.

Two more divers swam to the front of the small cylinder. A cap was removed and two hundred feet of wire pulled from inside. The divers then secured a three-foot antenna to the end. A small float bladder that surrounded the antenna hissed as it filled with air from the divers' regulators. They swam clear, then released it to float to the surface.

On the tug, Feroz lifted his handheld GPS and clicked the button to save the position. Then he reached for the tug's radio set, checked the frequency and spoke into the microphone. "This is navy tug *Hamoon*. This is navy tug *Hamoon*. Engine thrust bearing has lost oil pressure. We are stopped to make repairs."

"But, sir," worried the real master of the tug. "You broadcast in clear voice, no code."

"I know," Feroz rasped.

Around the gently bobbing tug, the divers two by two surfaced. In complete silence they slid back onto the tug's deck and disappeared into their hiding places.

When all were aboard, Feroz again picked up the microphone for the ship to shore radio. "This is navy tug *Hamoon*. We have made temporary repair to the engine, but cannot complete the mission. We are returning to base. Request a tug to assist with cargo."

USS MIAMI SSN 755
72 Miles off New York City

Grant McKinnon's crew needed every bit of skill they had to operate in shallow waters.

A 360-foot submarine submerged in 250 feet of water left no room for error. The ship's control party had to be on top of their game. Too much rudder and the bow would drop. A wrong push on the stern planes and the screw would hit the muddy bottom.

There had been a few close calls, but the crew seemed to be getting the hang of it. McKinnon was pleased.

Sonar could hear the P-3 Orion as it droned overhead. Except for the active sonar buoys dropped by the orbiting aircraft, it was quiet and peaceful. Quiet and peaceful did not make good sub-hunters or good submariners.

"Let's give 'em a workout," McKinnon growled. "Officer of the Deck, come to course 050. Use twenty degrees on the rudder. Ring up a full bell, if you please."

The improved Los Angles class submarine sprang forward like a filly out of a starting gate as the screw bit into the water. Skillfully, the helm and planes men kept the 6,900 ton submarine on an even keel as the rudder swung her to the new heading.

"Conn, Sonar," came a voice over the combat circuit 27MC. "They just went nuts up there. We're receiving active transmissions bearing 180 and 220."

"Probability of our detection?" McKinnon ordered over the open microphone.

"Not even close," the voice replied. "They're pinging on the cavitation when we went to full."

"Very well, Sonar," McKinnon smiled. "Officer of the Deck, all stop."

MIAMI slowed and again went as silent as the water that supported her hull.

"Conn, Sonar," whispered the voice over the 27MC. "Fly by east to west."

McKinnon smiled. "Good, someone up there has done their homework." He stepped to the chart. "Now, here's where we take the fly boys to school." He motioned for the Officer of the Deck to come to the chart. "See this?" He asked as he pointed to the chart. "That's a very large hole in the bottom. It goes down maybe five hundred feet. What we're going to do is sprint to the hole. When we get there, make your depth 300 feet."

Again, the screw dug and sliced into the ocean. Eight minutes later, MIAMI was in the hole. Above them, the P-3 blasted away with active sonar buoys.

"Now watch this," McKinnon grinned. "Make a circle using 15 degrees on the rudder."

As she answered the helm, the American submarine traced a huge arc around the underwater crater.

"Officer of the Deck," McKinnon ordered. "Ring up a one third bell, then creep out of the hole and get us back where we started."

Twenty minutes later, MIAMI was silently cruising alone.

"Sonar, Conn, what are the aircraft doing?" McKinnon asked.

"Conn, Sonar," the voice responded. "Still stuck in the hole, pinging away."

"You see guys," McKinnon said as he rested his hands on his hips. "We used a bottom feature to get away." He explained further. "We filled the hole with noise. The sound bounces off the bottom, off the sides. Then we went quiet and just slid out. Now the plane has so many contacts he's confused."

"Where did you learn that?" the Officer of the Deck asked.

McKinnon grinned. "Just made it up."

Chapter Nine

COUNTDOWN

"Malice drinks one-half of its own poison."
~Seneca

Iranian Naval Base, Bandar-E Abbas
January 1st

At midday, units of the Iranian Navy put to sea. Three aged, but well kept SAAM Class frigates took station 13 miles from the mouth of the harbor. Armed with Sea Cat anti-aircraft missiles and Limbo anti-submarine mortar launchers, the outdated ships provided the exercise area protection from intrusion.

Next, six French built COMBATTANTE II Class patrol boats rushed from the harbor. These small, but heavily armed ships, darted around in two formations of three.

Menacing and swift, these workhorses of the Iranian surface fleet wielded quite a punch. On each end of the thin hull sat deadly looking 76-mm OTO Melera canons. Along each vessels' centerline, six 25-foot Sistel Sea-Killer launch tubes angled at forty-degrees to each side.

Behind the darting patrol boats, the star attraction emerged from the mouth of the harbor. Towed behind two smoking tugs, the ex-American SUMMER Class Destroyer sloshed at the end of her tow line. Her guns and missiles removed, the rusted old ship seemed tired as she bobbed over the clear blue waters. The once proud American ship followed obediently to a point four miles from the entrance to Bandar-E Abbas. Once in position, anchor chains rattled loudly into the water, locking the old vessel to the sandy bottom.

When the sun began its descent over the Arabian Peninsula, all but two of the players were in place.

USS TEXAS SSN 755
30 Miles from Bandar-E Abbas

Commander Gracie checked various target plots on the Fire Control computer. So far, the Iranians had stayed inside their own waters.

The steady stream of information that flowed into the new attack submarine was good for training, but tactically useless.

What Gracie wanted was the Iranian KILO. The surface ships were little challenge, however, a modern submarine was another story, especially a modern diesel boat with a new torpedo.

Gracie, out of habit, looked at his own weapon status board. Eight tiny circular lights glowed cool green, indicating each of the tube-loaded ADCAP torpedoes was ready.

"We'll come up after dark," he announced. "See if we can get some IR pictures of these goobers."

He stepped into the Sonar Room. "You guys watch for the KILO. She should come out soon. Lot of noise up there, so sing out if you even think you hold her on the surface. It'll be harder if she pulls the plug and goes deep."

Moscow, Russia
The Kremlin

"**I do apologize**, Admiral Onufriev. It is a holiday," Vitenka offered.

Onufriev waved his hand as he sat at the small table across from Vitenka. "No need, Minister. My mother-in-law is visiting."

Vitenka smiled. "My condolences."

Onufriev's face turned serious. "Sir, I have looked over the data. I have also made some inquiries and managed to get some photographs. It is a puzzle. I have some of the pieces, but I do not know what the whole picture is to look like."

Vitenka's eyes narrowed. "You cannot know, Admiral. Please tell me what you have."

"First, the fifty workers," Onufriev started. "They are all skilled. These are not merely yard workers. I cannot believe they are there simply to repair the tanker."

"What would they be doing?" Vitenka asked.

Onufriev opened his briefcase. "I have here copies of a manifest for a large amount of ship grade steel plates." He handed the sheet to Vitenka. "As you can see, the manifest indicates the amount and size. At the bottom is the reason for the plates. Repair steering for tanker *Behzad Nabavi.*"

"Why would they need that much steel?" Vitenka asked. "The damage was reported to be minor."

"That I do not know, sir."

"What else?"

"The tanker," Onufriev said as he laid a photo on the table. "She is 280 meters by 57 meters. If you look here, the hull marker lines have been painted at 20 meters and again at 24 meters." With his thick finger he traced along the picture. "Here we have another set of markings at 106 meters and again at 112."

"Does this mean something?" Vitenka asked

Onufriev laid another photo on the table. "This is the submarine SIMCER. One of our Varshavyanka class sold to Iran in 1995."

"What the Americans call a KILO, yes?"

"Yes, Minister. Here she is moored near the tanker."

Vitenka scratched his chin. "I am not following."

"During the Great Patriotic War, Minister, the Italian Navy modified the tanker *Olterra* to launch midget submarines against the English. No one ever suspected it."

Vitenka leaned over the picture. "But a Varshavyanka is 80 meters long."

"It is, Minister," Onufriev nodded. "And it fits the lines marked on the tanker at 24 and 106 meters."

Vitenka digested this with his eyes fixed on the photo.

Onufriev cleared his throat, "What I believe is about to happen, Minister, is that the Iranians will use the tanker to get past this screen of American ships. Then the SIMCER will creep out undetected and strike the blow that will end, or at least deter America's presence in the Persian Gulf."

"What are you saying?" Vitenka barked.

Surprised by the Defense Minister's sudden irritation, Onufriev quickly placed another picture on the table. "This, Minister," he said as he tapped the photo. "It is the only target of interest to the Iranians, the USS RONALD REAGAN."

Vitenka grunted, "Ah yes, that obese aircraft carrier."

"It would be a mighty prize, Minister. Their naval exercise is planned for tomorrow," Onufriev continued. "That is when they will sneak the submarine into the tanker. At least, Minister, that is my... experienced guess. What I mean is, that is what I would do!"

"Very clever," Vitenka nodded. "Your people are attending to these maneuvers?"

"Of course, Minister, every second." The Admiral replied.

"I want a full report, as soon as possible."

"One more item, Minister," Onufriev leaned forward and whispered. "There is no new Iranian torpedo."

Harbor Control
Iranian Naval Base, Bandar-E Abbas
January 2nd

Iranian President Mehran stood as Commander Feroz stepped into the small room. "Commander, is everything ready?"

Feroz eyes narrowed as he studied the man. "Ready," he rasped.

"Today, we take the war to the enemy..."

Feroz lifted his hand as if to block the words. "I have no time for this."

"But..." The President spluttered.

"Save it for those who want to hear it."

Mehran's forced smile left his face. "You have a great lack of respect, Commander." The President stretched to his full height but stepped back when Feroz met his eyes. They said it all.

Mehran cleared his throat. "The device is tested?"

"All is ready."

"Are you sure the Americans will be

watching?"

SIMCER's Commanding Officer replaced his white peaked cap on his head. "I am. One or more of their submarines are out there."

"We have detected none!" Mehran countered.

"They are good at what they do," Feroz noted casually.

"How are we to know?"

"My guess would be an explosion."

"If they know..." He was again silenced by a look from Feroz.

"If they know, there will be more than one explosion."

Mehran tried to change the subject. "With success, you will return a hero to all who follow the one true God."

"With success, President, it is likely that when I return, you will be radioactive dust."

Mehran's eyes went wide. "They would not dare!"

"Ask the Japanese." Feroz growled as he turned toward the door.

The Iranian President now stood alone. Feroz's words hung like a foul cloud in the hot dry room.

11 Miles Off
Bandar-E Abbas

Three hundred feet above the gentle ripples of the Persian Gulf, four Falanga-M air target simulators raced toward the Iranian frigates.

Three of the turbo-fan driven drones simulated as best they could American FA-18 Fighter Bombers in the terminal phase of an attack.

Six miles from the ships, active radar seekers in each of the simulators' noses switched on.

On the first pulse of its radar, the lead Falanga detected and locked on the Frigate FARAMARZ.

A quarter mile away, the second and third simulators homed in on the ZAAL.

As programmed, the fourth Falanga-M climbed to 3000 feet and began a series of wide turns.

Within seconds, both frigates' Plessey AWS-1 radars detected the incoming simulated threat. In unison, the Iranian ships went to flank speed and began running a crossing pattern. The ships wove behind each other, attempting to confuse the drones' radar.

The tactic failed as the drones pressed on. At three miles, ZAAL fired a canister of chaff from her port launcher. A cloud of aluminum strips burst 110 meters off the ships quarter.

The third drone took the bait. It turned slightly away from the real target, and dove as it simulated a bomb run. ZAAL's RTN-10X Fire Control system instantly computed an intercept solution. A flash erupted from the forward end of the frigate. A thin finger of smoke jabbed toward the sky as a Sea Cat missile left the launch rail. Three seconds later, a fireball blasted the drone from the air.

FARAMARZ"'s Sea Cat system could not lock onto either of the two remaining targets.

At one mile, the ship's Mk 8 duel purpose gun swung toward the threat. Four sharp reports echoed off the water. The 114mm radar fused shells burst around the simulated attacker. Two left black puffs of heavy smoke behind the drone and one in front. The last exploded inside the Falanga-M's fuel cell. The drone seemed to fold up inside a sheet of flame as it tumbled into the sea.

At 1,000 feet, the fourth drone turned in lazy circles as it simulated the pattern of an American EC-2 HAWKEYE Early Warning Aircraft.

As her sisters engaged the phantom FA-18s, the third Iranian frigate, ROSTAM, gained contact on the high-level target. At a range of two miles, a Standard Missile roared from the frigate's modified launcher. Nine seconds later, an ugly smudge of orange and black marked the end of the drone's mission.

USS TEXAS SSN 775

"Sonar, Conn. We hold gunfire and explosions bearing 030."

"Conn, Sonar aye," Commander Gracie acknowledged. "That correlates to our visuals."

"Conn, ESM," announced an excited voice over the speaker. "Gain new IJ2 Band contact, bearing 322. Contact designated Romeo-23, classified as Snoop Tray surface search and navigation radar carried on Iranian submarines."

"ESM, Conn aye," Commander Gracie replied calmly. "Okay, Sonar, pick him out of that traffic jam."

PIER 14
Iranian Naval Base, Bandar-E Abbas

Twenty minutes after SIMCER cast off her lines, the tanker *Behzad Nabavi* eased into the narrow channel. Seven stories above the tanker's waterline, an Iranian Naval Officer paced her bridge. Dressed in civilian clothes, he leaned over the wing rail. "I've never operated a ship this big," he murmured to his First Officer.

"What is our destination?"

"Venezuela."

"Why?"

"I do not know."

The First Officer grabbed the rail tightly. "We have no orders?"

"Oh, we have orders."

As the channel widened, the crew on the tanker's deck waved at those along the docks.

Two of the sailors gave the thumbs up when they saw a man on the pier raise a camera to his face. They had no idea the picture would be in Moscow within the hour.

USS TEXAS SSN 775

Sixty feet below the surface, TEXAS slipped unheard in a tight racetrack pattern eight miles from the Iranian fleet. The action on the surface created a confused, chaotic mass of noise. Older passive systems would have had problems sorting treasure from trash.

TEXAS had no such problem as a faint signal nudged at the passive wide aperture array along her hull. Computers filtered and washed the sound in milliseconds. Bearing and signal to noise information flashed across LCD screens in her Sonar Room.

"Conn, Sonar gained new passive broadband contact, designate Sierra 41. We hold contact on tracker 2. One five bladed screw making 45 RPM. Classified contact as surfaced Russian built diesel submarine."

"Very well, Sonar," Gracie nodded, grinning fiercely as he scanned the screen. "Attention Tracking Party, Sierra 41 is the contact of interest. Designate Sierra 41 as Master 1." He took a deep breath "Track Master 1."

Chapter Ten

SHOWTIME

"Man is the only kind of varmint that sets his own trap, baits it, then steps in it."
~John Steinbeck, Sweet Thursday

Naval Submarine Base
Groton, Connecticut
January 2nd

Patches of blue showed through dark gray puffs of clouds as MIAMI made the sharp turn into her assigned berth. Here and there, rays of sunlight struck the ground like beams from a flashlight, as if to challenge the ice and cold.

At his place in the submarine's bridge, Grant McKinnon hoped the few days at sea had done as much for him as it had for MIAMI's crew. Tonight, he would again be alone, just him and the old house.

Minutes later, lines from the pier snaked over her decks where sailors slipped the looped ends to the fixed and retractable cleats along her round hull.

The tide, rushing up the Thames River, caused the 6,900 ton American submarine to pull at hcr lines as if she was some wild captured animal.

"Officer of the Deck, secure the maneuvering watch and set the normal in port watch section." McKinnon ordered as he stepped down the ladder.

"Captain," the young officer said as he nudged McKinnon's arm, "Group Six is headed this way."

McKinnon peeked over the rim of the bridge. The unmistakable form of his Commanding Officer bounded down the strip of cement like a force of nature.

Unless a boat returned from a major deployment, the Admiral stayed up on the hill. Suddenly a twinge of hope shivered up McKinnon's spine. *Maybe a deployment for me*, he thought as he watched him march down the pier.

"Better see what's going on," McKinnon muttered as he slid down the bridge hatch ladder.

MIAMI's Captain made it to the pier just as Admiral Tarrent arrived. He saluted. "Good to see you, Admiral."

Tarrent's face remained fixed in a scowl as he returned the salute. "Come with me,

Commander." Tarrent turned toward the end of the pier.

"What's wrong?" McKinnon asked cautiously.

"Keep this under your hat," Tarrent half whispered.

"Of course."

"We have a problem with base security," Tarrent huffed as the two men stepped through the gate. "This way," he gestured. "About three hours ago, two people asked to get on base." Tarrent led MIAMI's confused Captain toward his car. "Base Security called my office when it happened. Thought I needed to handle this one myself."

McKinnon looked over his shoulder at MIAMI. "Terrorists?" He asked quietly.

Ten feet short of the car, Tarrent stopped. "One is for sure. Wait here."

Again, McKinnon turned toward the waterfront. Four other submarines rested at adjacent piers. He strained his eyes. No additional watches prowled the waterfront. No armored cars patrolled. He stood confused.

"Hello, you ol' pirate," a tiny voice said from behind him.

McKinnon spun on his heels as Misty launched herself from the back of Admiral Tarrent's car. The sheer surprise sent a bolt through his head. McKinnon's jaw fell open.

She ran to him. Her heavy pink and blue snowsuit swished as her tiny legs carried her.

He scooped her up. "What are you doing

here?"

"I missed you," she giggled.

McKinnon's mind almost overloaded as Jennifer slid from the seat. "Hey, Sailor," she smiled.

"I... don't understand?" He stuttered.

"I saw your boat," Misty said. "Mr. Tarry said you were in the sail. I didn't see any sails." She put her mouth close to his ear. "Does he know what he's talking about?"

Admiral Tarrent rolled his eyes. "That one," he said nodding at Misty. "Is the terrorist."

McKinnon looked again into Jennifer's eyes. "Why are you here?"

Tarrent turned back toward the pier. "I'm going to see Captain Morse over at MOTU. I'll be back in a bit."

Jennifer smiled as she pushed her red hair from her face. "Misty likes it here. I do too. So why not?"

"I don't know what to say," McKinnon managed.

"Can we see your boat?" Misty asked.

Iranian Frigate
FARAMARZ

BBC reporter, Kevin Osprey and his cameraman, Stewart Miles braced against the thin aluminum superstructure as the small warship heeled in a sharp port turn.

Miles had some great footage of the Iranian

ships in action. Both men had covered conflicts from Sri-Lanka to Iraq. It was not difficult to tell these exercises were canned events. Thus far, this assignment had not been very exciting. Still, Osprey smiled and congratulated the frigate's crew.

"You have good pictures?" The Iranian Weapons Officer asked proudly.

"Oh, yes," Osprey smiled.

"We now proceeding to main event," the Weapons Officer said with a nod toward a black shape off the frigate's starboard side.

"That ship?" Miles asked.

"You must have plenty films. Our submarine will sink it with torpedo attack."

"Now that is news!" Osprey grinned.

Miles wiped the lens of his camera again, and checked the footage meter.

"After this, America will fear any attack on us," the young officer crowed.

Iranian Submarine
SIMCER

Hidden deep in her hull, the diesel engines rumbled softly as they both propelled the small ship and charged her batteries. Her rounded unglamorous bow lifted and fell in the gentle swells. A mist of warm salt-water fell gently over the five men standing in the cramped cockpit of the Russian built submarine.

100 meters aft on the after port quarter, a

large RIB type boat bounced along as it rode the submarine's wake.

Feroz wiped the salt spray from his face. "Clear the bridge," he ordered.

Now alone, Feroz turned toward the inflatable in his submarine's wake. He lifted his hand over his head, then lowered it slowly.

Feroz had to squint to see the return signal. He took his last look at the sun, before he climbed heavily down the ladder.

USS TEXAS SSN 775

"Conn, Sonar, Master 1 is venting tanks," Sonar reported.

"Very well, Sonar," Commander Gracie acknowledged. "Okay, boys, let's see what these guys can do."

Almost at the same second, another report came in. "Conn, Sonar, gained new passive broadband contact. Submerged contact is a 78 Hertz tonal on the same bearing as the KILO."

"Stay on it," Gracie ordered. "She's submerged."

Iranian Submarine
SIMCER

At 200 feet, the small submarine leveled off. Free of the surface and now on her batteries, SIMCER was but a whisper of noise.

Feroz ordered 2 knots. Carefully, the small

boat shifted slight amounts of water until the KILO was in perfect balance.

Inside SIMCER, only the glow of screens and instruments provided light. In the dark of the control center Feroz whispered to the officers gathered nervously around the plot table "Do you have any questions?" He asked as he searched the dim faces. "None? Then, we begin."

Despite SIMCER's ungainly form, she was nimble even at low speeds. Feroz turned the ship in a sweeping 360 degrees. Satisfied with his position, he ordered his boat to periscope depth.

USS TEXAS SSN 775

The new attack submarine hovered at periscope depth. Commander Gracie looked at the greenish waterfall display of the passive sonar. The Iranian submarine was a faint light green line that slowly descended to the bottom of the screen. "Looks like our boy is clearing his baffles," He said as he tapped the screen. A sudden flicker of light caught his eye. "Sonar, what's that new trace in the upper DE?"

"Conn, Sonar. New contact passive broadband tracker 9. New contact bears 098. Designate new contact Sierra 29. Contact classified merchant by nature of sound. Contact is making 34 RPM on two five-bladed screws."

"Somebody screwed up," Gracie laughed.

"Big ole fat tanker right in the middle of their war game."

"Conn, ESM. Picking up some clear voice comms, from the same bearing as Sierra 29."

"You have any idea what they are talking about?" Gracie asked.

"Conn, ESM, no, but from the tone someone's getting their butt munched."

Again, Commander Gracie chuckled, "Conn, ESM, aye."

Iranian Frigate
FARAMARZ

We are near the test site," the young Iranian officer explained. "From here you can see the target. We have set up a speaker so you can also hear underwater communications with our submarine."

BBC reporter Kevin Osprey cocked his head. "I don't speak Farsi."

"No worry," the officer smiled. "I am here to translate." He nodded toward the doomed old destroyer. "Be ready with the camera."

Iranian Submarine
SIMCER

Water fell away like a curtain from the optic window of SIMCER's slim attack periscope. Commander Feroz pressed his scarred face to the rubber eyepiece. Quickly, he rotated the

EPITAPH 119

scope to the bearing of the target ship. "Weapons ready?" he asked.

"Set."

'Target now bearing 120. Range 990 meters. Target presents port 20 angle on the bow." Feroz lined up on the target. Then he moved the scope 40 degrees to port where his real target bobbed unseen in the mild chop of the Persian Gulf.

"System ready, Captain," the Weapons Officer reported.

"Flood tube three and open outer door," Feroz ordered. "Stand by for firing observation.

USS TEXAS SSN 775

"Conn, Sonar, we hold metallic transients from Master-1. Tube flooding noise and tube door coming open."

"Very well, Sonar," Gracie replied calmly. "Stay cool in there," he urged.

Iranian Submarine
SIMCER

Feroz swung the periscope around. "Range clear," he announced. "Navigator, inform the range ship we are about to attack."

Iranian Frigate
FARAMARZ

"What is he saying?" Osprey asked.

"He states the range is safe and he will now attack the target," the officer replied.

Osprey tapped his cinematographer's shoulder. "Start rolling."

Iranian Submarine
SIMCER

"Stand by in three... two... one... launch," Feroz ordered.

Inside the tube, the ET-80A torpedo felt the sudden voltage that surged into the power control unit.

A quick self-test told the torpedo that it was indeed in water, that it did have a search plan, and that the tube door was opened.

Three gyros used the power to spin up and align themselves with the earth and the course they were to steer. In milliseconds, a computer gathered all the information, and checked off items as they came in. Satisfied the information was within parameters of its stored launch criteria, the computer flashed two signals along dedicated circuits.

One pulse traveled through the weapon along the thin titanium guidance wire. This signal caused a light on the weapon guidance console to glow green. It told the Weapons Officer the wire was ready to transmit and receive signals.

The second pulse traveled through the

thumb thick umbilical linked to the tube door.

One machine talked to another, the torpedo telling the ship it was ready to go.

Valves rolled open. High-pressure air pushed against a piston housed in a cylinder located under the torpedo tubes. As the pressure moved the piston, a column of water surged from the sea up into the tube. Pressure built around the after end of the waiting weapon.

The pressure squared a second later and forced the weapon into the sea.

USS TEXAS SSN 775

"Conn, Sonar, we hold launch transients," the Sonar Supervisor announced. A second later, "Torpedo in the water," crackled over the 27MC.

"Call it out," Commander Gracie ordered.

There was a nervous silence. "Sonar?" Gracie asked.

"Uh, Sonar, Conn, based on engine lines, this torpedo is classified as Russian built ET-80. Not a new weapon."

"What?" Gracie asked. He looked up at the green line rapidly tracing along the screen.

"Conn, Sonar, this profile shows a standard run to enable. Weapon at estimated 40 knots on the left drawing left."

Gracie stood confused. "What's going on?"

Iranian Submarine
SIMCER

"Normal launch," noted the Weapon's Officer. "We have communications with the weapon."

SIMCER went to 80 meters while in a soft banking turn to starboard. "Range to target?"

"600 hundred meters," Sonar reported.

"Enable weapon," Feroz ordered. "Helm, come to course 168."

On the weapons control console, a button was pushed. A 44-Hertz signal raced along the six miles of wire that connected the torpedo with SIMCER. A thousandth of a second later, the torpedo's brain received the order.

From the nose of the torpedo, a high-pitched ping echoed into the ocean.

"Weapon enabled." Unseen in the dark, SIMCER's Weapons Officer sent the weapon new orders.

USS TEXAS SSN 775

"What do you see, Sonar?" Commander Gracie asked. The bright green line on the waterfall display had suddenly changed direction.

There was a pause. "Sonar, Conn, there is a doppler shift on the torpedo." Another long pause hung in the cool air of the American submarine. "Conn, it... wait."

Gracie needed no confirmation. He could see it on the display in front of his face. "Oh my

God!"

"Conn, Sonar, circular run on Master-1's weapon. Weapon went active and turned on the firing ship."

"Stay calm in there," Gracie urged. "Give me the reports."

"Conn, Sonar, Master-1 has increased speed. I hold blade tip cavitation."

"Is Master-1 maneuvering?"

"Conn, Sonar, Master-1 is turning."

Iranian Submarine
SIMCER

"Helm 180," Feroz ordered, "increase speed to 18 knots. Diving Control, come to 130 meters then 30 meters."

The Russian built KILO obeyed at once. Those of her crew not seated held on as the small submarine turned and rose at the same time.

"Where is the weapon?" Feroz asked.

"Torpedo is in our baffles, bearing 170. Range to weapon 400 meters and gaining," the Weapons Officer replied with a slight smile.

"Good," Feroz rasped. "Keep it there." SIMCER's Captain looked down at the digital counter of the inertia navigation system. "Helm left to 348."

Iranian Frigate
FARAMARZ

Though he did not understand, BBC reporter Kevin Osprey noted the tone in the voice from the speaker. "What did he say?" He asked.

Out of habit, cameraman Miles turned the camera on the young Iranian officer. It was difficult to get a good focus with his lens set for distance. Still the nervous look on the officer's face was photojournalism gold.

"Ah... there seems to be a problem," he stammered as he listened to the voice from the speaker.

"What kind of problem?" Osprey asked politely.

The officer's smile faded as Miles documented the man's search for words.

"The weapon has malfunctioned," he said in a strained whisper. "It seems to be after our submarine."

Iranian Submarine SIMCER

"Range?" Feroz barked.

"200 meters."

"Keep it close," Feroz rasped through clenched teeth. "Another twenty seconds."

Feroz again checked the dead reckoning plot he had carefully laid out. "Helm, steady on new course 020."

USS TEXAS SSN 775

"Captain, the weapon has acquired Master-1. I

hold three active returns," the Sonar Supervisor reported.

Commander Gracie swallowed hard. "They're going to die," he whispered. He looked at the passive sonar waterfall display. The bright green line wiggled this way, then that in perfect unison, and closed quickly with the faint line of the KILO.

"Must have broken the guide wire," Gracie reasoned. "They can't shut it down."

"Conn, Sonar, estimate impact in ten seconds."

Iranian Submarine
SIMCER

"Bring the weapon along side, then shut it down on my mark," Asha Feroz ordered.

"Range 50 meters," the weapons officer called out.

Feroz picked up the ship-wide address system. "Brace," he called out.

"Range 30 meters."

"Sonar ready on the fathometer?" Feroz rasped.

"Ready," a voice replied from the dark.

"Range 10 meters."

Feroz waited three seconds. "All stop, lock the screw. Shut the weapon down. Go active, one active pulse on the fathometer."

Feroz had done better than he thought possible. SIMCER was 100 meters from the old boiler that lay on the bottom.

In the RIB boat the faint pulse of the fathometer was heard by one of Feroz's hand-picked commandos. Instantly, he pressed a button on a small radio transmitter.

The antenna that bobbed 50 meters away easily received the signal from the transmitter. It pulsed down the wire to the metallic cylinder clamped to the old boiler.

There, the signal energized a battery powered relay. The relay felt the tingle of voltage and shut. As the tiny contacts of the relay met, the stored energy of a capacitor flashed to an explosive charge the same weight and consistency of an ET-80A torpedo.

The energy of the explosion tore open the case of the old boiler, then superheated gasses filled the space evaporating the water in nanoseconds. Though built of high grade steel the boiler was unable to resist the stress. It erupted in an expanding geyser of steam and molten metal.

Shielded from the brunt of the explosion by the rounded shape of the boiler, SIMCER slid quietly by, pushed forward by kinetic energy.

USS TEXAS SSN 775

A solemn voice now broadcast over the 27MC, "Conn, Sonar, loud explosion and breaking up noises on the bearing of Master-1."

Commander Gracie stood in shock. He stared at the sonar display even as the bright green flash subsided.

"Very well," he muttered. "Sonar, backup all data." He leaned against the stainless steel rail that surrounded the Conn. "Have the communicator draft a SITREP. Officer of the Deck, go deep, come to course 030. We need to clear the datum and phone this one in."

Chapter Eleven

BAIT AND SWITCH

*"Silence is the true friend
that never betrays."*
~Confucius

Groton Heights, Connecticut
January 2nd

"This is it," Jennifer said as she gestured proudly.

Grant McKinnon looked around at the living room of the two-story wood and brick house. "Not bad," he smiled. "Those windows let in a lot of light."

"Come see my room," Misty said as she tugged on McKinnon's arm.

"Run on up and I'll be there in a second," he smiled down.

"Okay, but you better hurry," she frowned.

McKinnon watched as she carefully climbed

the stairs of polished oak. When she was out of sight, Grant leaned against the rail. "Tell me something."

"Sure," Jennifer replied.

"Why?"

Jennifer lifted her chin as if trying to find the right words. "Misty's not the only one who missed you. She never stopped talking about you. Then one night when I put her to bed, we talked for an hour about you." Jennifer pushed her finger lightly into his chest. "She said you were cute for an old man."

"But..." McKinnon stammered.

"That night, I realized I couldn't get you out of my head either. I've always taken chances. It's my nature," Jennifer said with a shrug of her shoulders. "Some have paid off, while others... well." She tucked her long red hair behind her ears. "So, I'm taking another chance. If it works out like I hope, then fine. If not... well, at least I can tell myself I tried."

McKinnon felt himself flush and his blood turn hot in his veins. He wanted to take this woman in his arms. Then a vision of Cathy drifted into his mind.

Guilt cooled the blood, as his mind reacted to what was now and what was memory. Part of his brain begged him to leave, while another told him to stay.

Iranian Submarine
SIMCER

The KILO took the force of the blast well. Other than a power generating static converter that tripped offline and a small leak in the diesel exhaust muffler flange, there was no damage.

Gently, the 2,350 ton submarine settled on the sandy bottom. Now, Feroz had only to wait.

Iranian Frigate
FARAMARZ

From 100 meters, a plume of angry water shot high above the frigate's mainmast. As the water fell, black ugly mounds of the seabed bubbled to the surface before they too subsided.

Kevin Osprey clenched the rail so hard the feeling left his fingers. "Miles, did you get that?"

The cameraman was silent, his eye pressed into the viewfinder. He swung the camera left to where the young Iranian officer stood in shock. He triggered the zoom, the lens focused clearly on tears that streamed down the dark skin of the young man's face.

The voice from the speaker became frantic. Alarms rang and suddenly, the frigate gained speed.

Camouflaged, heavily armed speedboats appeared. They crossed in front and behind of the frigate, each on a course for the fountain of bubbles that still boiled off the frigate's side.

Miles panned over the scene. Chaos was always good news. Now at speed, a mist of spray lifted over FARAMARZ's bow.

The sheet of water droplets fell gently over the deck and camera lens. Miles was reaching for the lens cloth tucked in his shirt pocket when he noticed a black form drawing closer.

He knew little of ships, however, he did know that all mariners are supposed to render aid when a ship was in trouble. With the lens once again clear, he put the camera back to his shoulder and fingered the record button.

The Pentagon
Washington D.C.

Chairman of the Joint Chiefs of Staff, Admiral Malroy, glanced over his handwritten notes. He had long since given up attempts to remember all the points he needed to make.

These weekly video speeches would find their way to most major commands in the United States Military. Malroy sometimes wondered aloud to his staff if anyone really watched the tapes. "If I had my choice of movies, it sure wouldn't be some grumpy old man telling you how important it is that you're sitting neck deep in camel crap, then asking you to re-enlist."

Somewhere off to the side, one of the Navy Media Crew switched on a stage light. Malroy flinched at the glare.

"Sorry, sir," the Media Supervisor offered. "We need to light your best side."

"My best side?" Malroy sneered. "Here, let

me turn around."

The digital video camera facing his desk stood alone on its tripod like some one-eyed alien from another planet.

Again, Malroy reviewed his notes. "Need to get this in one take," he announced to the bustling media crew. "Got the grandkids coming in from Mayport."

Marine Corps Major Randy Desota brushed past the light technician.

"Sir," he bent down to the Admiral's ear.

"Hello, Major," Malroy said warmly, glad for the interruption.

"Admiral, we need you in the conference room," Desota said quietly.

Malroy let his notes fall to the desk. "Now? What is it?"

Desota looked around to be sure no one could hear. "There's been an incident in the Persian Gulf."

Malroy looked into the Marine's eyes. "Bad?" he asked.

"Yes, sir."

Iranian Frigate
FARAMARZ

BBC reporter, Kevin Osprey, was careful. Eye contact and body language meant as much as words. "Are you sure it's all right to continue filming?" He asked.

"Yes, yes, you have permission," the young

Iranian officer nodded.

"May I interview you also?"

The officer stopped. "I must get permission for that."

"All right," Osprey turned to his camera man and winked, "Miles, let's do our story right here." The reporter then switched on the tiny microphone fitted into a buttonhole in his open necked shirt.

Miles pivoted the camera toward Osprey, checked the focus, then lifted his finger.

"In three-two-one... This is Kevin Osprey onboard an Iranian warship somewhere in the Persian Gulf. We have witnessed a terrible accident that has seen the destruction of one of Iran's three front line submarines. What we know from our Iranian hosts is that a new torpedo launched from the submerged submarine SIMCER, turned back and struck the submarine. We ourselves witnessed a tremendous undersea explosion. Units of the Iranian navy are now in a desperate, but I am told hopeless, search for survivors."

A stream of navy men suddenly ran past the BBC team. They stopped just forward of the frigate's funnel. One pointed to the water near the warship's side.

Miles slowly spun the camera around to follow the action. He panned over the water to where the man was pointing.

Bodies were bobbing there in a froth of red water. One was face down, arms extended over the head, the light blue jumpsuit of the Iranian submarine service all but blown away, exposing a shattered pelvis. Both lower legs were gone, with only nubs of bone visible.

The second body seemed intact. This one floated face up. Small holes pocked along the jumpsuit like brown-ringed craters. A burn just under the armpit showed up a dirty black.

Through the magnified eye of the camera, Miles could see the man's eyes were open, his face as if recording the sudden pain of his own death. Miles looked away from the image.

"Keep filming," Osprey hissed.

The Pentagon
Washington, D.C.

"So, what we have," Admiral Malroy began, "as of an hour ago, is an Iranian submarine blasting itself to kingdom come."

Around the table, heads nodded in agreement.

"CNO, how close were our forces?" Malroy asked.

"120 miles," the Chief of Naval Operations replied. "We pulled back when they announced their exercises."

"Submarines?"

"TEXAS is now 50 miles from the Iranian base. She's still undetected."

Malroy sighed. "Of course, they'll blame us."

"What happened?" Readiness Commander and Marine Corps General Clarence Hardik asked.

Malroy lifted his palms. "You folks over at Fort Meade know anything about a new Iranian torpedo?"

"No, sir," Captain Ellen Knotts of Naval Intelligence spoke up. "The only thing we can think of is the Iranians tried to modify a Russian weapon. Probably screwed around in the guidance unit."

Malroy rubbed at his neck. "My great grandfather was a watchmaker. He used to say the only two people who took the back off a fine timepiece were watchmakers and fools."

"Sir, this may be a chance at some really useful information," Knotts said.

Malroy's eyebrows lifted. "How so, Captain?"

"The Iranians don't have any real salvage capabilities. They'll send divers down, and accomplish little. We, on the other hand..."

"Are you suggesting we attempt salvage?" The Chief of Naval Operations interrupted.

"Of course not!" Knotts said with a wave of her hand. "But a look at the sub might be of interest."

"How so?" The CNO asked.

Knotts leaned forward in her chair. "If the Iranians did monkey with their torpedoes, others might be lying around on the bottom. We might also be able to see how the sub died. What are the structural weaknesses in the KILO class?"

"How would you get that type of information? We can't send a ship in there," the

CNO argued.

"No, but a SEAL team could get in, snap some pictures. DALLAS is in theater. She could do it."

Malroy looked down at the table. "That's taking a mighty big risk."

Knotts smiled. "Admiral, when I graduated from the Academy, the guest speaker told us to think outside the box. He said something like grabbing at straws might seem a waste... unless you happen to get the right straw."

"I really think this is a bad idea," the CNO protested.

"Let me see, who was that speaker?" Knotts continued, rubbing her chin.

Malroy chuckled. "It was me. I make lousy speeches." He leaned back in his chair. The eyes of everyone in the room focused on him. "Okay, we'll judge Iranian reaction. If possible, send in the SEALS. CNO, get your people in contact with Knott's folks. I'll brief the Secretary and the President."

Iranian Submarine
SIMCER

In the silence of the dark control center, Commander Feroz stared at the sonar display.

"Captain, the tanker has started and is on course," the Sonar Officer reported.

"Pump 4000 liters to sea," Feroz ordered.

As quietly as she had settled, the KILO class

submarine lifted from the bottom.

Iranian Frigate
FARAMARZ

Cautious to stay out of the way, BBC reporter, Kevin Osprey watched as the bodies landed on the frigate's deck. He had seen bodies before, but there was something not quite right about these.

The dead men's heads were shaved close, not like the sailors around him whose hair was rather long.

He noted the uniforms. Other than damage by the blast, the material seemed new. Neither the officers nor the crew men who handled the bodies seemed interested in any identification.

Every Iranian sailor Osprey had seen since this assignment began wore dog tags. The bodies laid out on the hot steel deck had none.

Now the corpses had been covered with gray woolen blankets.

Iranian Submarine
SIMCER

"Tanker is above us, Captain," the Sonar Officer reported.

"Up 'scope," Feroz barked.

Quickly, the silver barrel of the attack scope lifted from its well. Feroz twisted the handle until the optics pointed toward the smooth surface. He panned around. "There she is," he whispered.

Above SIMCER, the giant hull of the tanker blocked the sunlight. Suddenly, a string of faint flashing bulbs lit up a long rectangular area of the tanker's bottom.

With quick, yet minute use of her screw and rudder, SIMCER hovered directly under the waiting tanker.

"Navigator, check set and drift," Feroz ordered. "Diving Officer, start the trim pump. Pump to my mark, low speed."

Through the periscope's optic window, Feroz saw the opening cut neatly in the tanker's bottom. He swept the scope fore and aft as he checked his position. If either vessel was even a meter off the mark, SIMCER would smash into the thin-hulled oil tanker.

SIMCER rose slowly. "Keep pumping," Feroz urged. Then the view in the scope went black. "Lower scope," he ordered. "We are in."

Feroz had positioned the small submarine perfectly. Atmospheric pressure kept most of the seawater from entering the neatly cut hole in the tanker's storage hold.

In the dark, Feroz's men climbed quickly to the casing. Flashlights stabbed at the dark, dank interior.

In the overhead 50 feet above their heads, rows of fluorescent bulbs flickered on. The shell nearly 300 feet long and 80 feet wide was like a small building inside the tanker's hull.

Steel I-beams anchored to the rounded

double hull of the tanker's bottom supported a structure of three decks on each side. Ladders and narrow stairs criss-crossed the decks.

Flimsy aluminum doors gave access to various rooms and compartments. On the top deck, a small round hatch jutted from the steel wall. A long strip of steel welded on arched steel supports provided a walkway next to the now surfaced submarine.

Fumes from the fresh coat of white primer hung in the thick hot air.

SIMCER's crew spread into the shell. Three electrical technicians raced to the second deck port side. They tugged at an umbilical paid out along the small pier. The cable fed over the side and coupled to the submarine's power receptacle.

Six diesel mechanics checked the seven massive pumps. If needed, they would keep the water in the shell level with the water outside the tanker's hull.

Others scaled ladders high above the submarine. These men removed large pins from the lock arms. Electric chain hoists whined as these arms slowly lowered over SIMCER's hull.

Constructed of lattice-braced steel, the arms descended until they sat neatly on the KILO's deck. At the end of them, clamps fitted on pivot points and operated by a three-inch thick threaded rod pushed into and locked inside the submarines limber holes. Ratchets echoed in the humid heat. With the clamps tight, SIMCER and the tanker were one.

Chapter Twelve

DECISIONS

"Choices are the hinges of destiny."
~Edwin Markham

Ministry of Defense
The Kremlin
Moscow, Russia
January 3rd

The pictures, still warm from the printer, were passed quickly into the Minister's office.

Admiral Onufriev's knee nervously twitched as he studied the high-resolution images. "Sir, this is proof."

Defense Minister Zivon Vitenka leaned closer. "Tell me what you see."

"Here," Onufriev said. "That can only be the exhaust for a generator. For an oil tanker, there is no need for power this far forward."

"I see. However, four bodies were recovered."

"Yes, Minister," Onufriev nodded. "We have the footage from the BBC. My concern is the conditions of those bodies. You and I know what submariners look like."

"Yes, we do," Vitenka sighed. "However, Admiral, ask yourself if this evidence would hold up at the UN."

Onufriev sat back. "Minister, if this is true, the United Nations will not have time to act."

"I agree." Vitenka gathered the pictures into a brown folder.

"Will you inform the Americans?" Onufriev asked.

"There are elements to this you do not and cannot know," the Minister of Defense whispered without meeting the Onufriev's eyes. "Your service has been invaluable. You are dismissed."

With the Admiral gone, Vitenka sat staring out the window where shades of night were creeping in, smothering the light of day. Wearily, he picked up the phone.

Iranian Naval Base, Bandar-E Abbas

"We have searched all we can," the diver explained.

"The surface search was also negative," another Iranian officer reported.

Admiral Dareh took in a deep lungful of humid air. "There were supposed to be five bodies. I need five bodies."

>6
6

"Sharks, perhaps?" The diver offered.

"We can only hope," Dareh hissed.

Groton Heights
Connecticut

"This has to be the last one," Grant McKinnon huffed as he lowered the cardboard box marked DISHES to the smooth tile floor.

"It'll be worth it," Jennifer smiled. "You're getting a home-cooked meal out of it."

McKinnon tried to remember the last time someone had cooked for him. "That does sound good."

Jennifer placed the last sheet of shelf paper in the cabinet. "What about tomorrow?"

"Tomorrow?"

"Yes, what would you like? Tonight is fried chicken."

"Well..."

"Your choice," she nodded. "Start handing me the glasses."

McKinnon stared at Jennifer as she worked. Even in her faded jeans and worn flannel shirt and no makeup, she was beautiful. Without his brain being allowed to vote on the matter, Grant wrapped his arms around her slender waist and brought his lips to hers.

He'd expected resistance, but received none. She burrowed into him. Her soft lips warm and wonderful. Once again, the guilt rattled through his mind, breaking the spell. He pulled away.

"I'm sorry," he blushed. "That was... wrong."

"Wrong? Why?" Jennifer asked as she took his hand in hers.

"I'm just... I mean there are things about me you don't know."

Jennifer's eyes softened. "I... I know about your wife and your son," she said gently. "I understand."

"How could you?" McKinnon asked.

Jennifer's lips curled into a rich grin.

McKinnon's mind put the pieces together. "Burke Tarrent!"

Jennifer nodded. "You're like a son to him," she murmured as she moved against him and laid her head on his chest.

"You mean he just told you my life story," McKinnon muttered.

"Not exactly," she giggled. "When we came to the base looking for you, he sat me down and had what he called 'A come to Jesus talk' with me."

"That's Burke all right," McKinnon laughed.

"He told me about you and asked what my intentions were. I felt like I was in high school."

"Sorry about that," McKinnon grunted.

"Don't be. It was really quite sweet," she kissed his chin. "He cares a lot about you... and so do I."

Aboard the Iranian Oil Tanker
Behzad Nabavi
70 Miles off Al Ghaydah, Yemen

Air inside the steel cavern hung hot and heavy. Every breath the men took reeked of rotted bilge debris, uncured epoxy paint, oil and stale sewage.

Feroz allowed the upper hatch of the shell opened briefly for ventilation. An eight-inch pipe connected by a flex hose to a cone shaped inlet pierced the tanker's deck three meters behind the kingpost, vented the foul air.

The hatch could not remain open long. Air pressure escaped from the hole, and allowed the sea to rush in at the bottom. The huge pumps could keep up with the flow for only thirty minutes at a time.

On the top deck near the hatch, a small chamber constructed of light steel sheets, and furnished with a scarred wooden table and rusted folding chairs acted as Feroz's stateroom. On the rough bulkhead, an old rotary telephone allowed communication to and from *Behzad Nabavi's* bridge.

"What is your speed?" Feroz asked. "Maintain that," he ordered. "Any patrol aircraft near us?" He wiped the salt and sweat from his face on his sleeve. "Good. Keep your eyes open."

VEPR K-157
Lapadnaya Lista
Russian Submarine Base

Lieutenant Shurgatov rapped gently at the Captain's door. Lately, Danyankov seemed a changed man, but who knew how long that would last. The Lieutenant determined it would not be he who broke whatever spell had blessed them so far.

"Enter," Danyankov said pleasantly enough.

Shurgatov carefully opened the door the way a man might open the lid of a coffin. "Sir, Captain Lebedko from headquarters is on the pier."

"Why didn't you invite him down?" Danyankov asked without looking up from the paperwork on his cramped desk.

"I did, Sir. He says he must speak to you alone."

VEPR's Commander looked up from his work. "Is that all he said?"

"It is, Captain," the Lieutenant replied.

"Must be important," Danyankov said softly. "Inform him I will be there directly."

"Yes, sir," Shurgatov nodded.

Valerik Danyankov got to his feet and wrestled into his long bridge coat, then placed the furry Ushanka hat squarely on his head.

Headquarters delivering my transfer orders in person. What a nice touch! He grunted as he climbed up the cold steel ladder.

USS DALLAS SSN 700
The Red Sea
One Mile off the Dahlak Archipelago

In the shelter of tiny islands that dotted the area, DALLAS pushed up through the dark warm sea. In the late 90's, DALLAS traded in her role as hunter-killer for that of a Special Forces delivery platform. On the long rounded after deck, the dry dock shelter sat like an ugly growth. The shelter held the SEAL's own small submarine, as well as other items needed by the elite team.

With little more than a swish, DALLAS rose to the surface. She showed no lights, and remained trimmed low in the water. Her black lusterless hull blended with the night and the islands behind her.

The gently lapping waves silenced the whir of a muffled outboard engine. Those on DALLAS's dark bridge turned toward the swish of the boats wake. It appeared as if out of thin air. It rounded the tip of one of the nameless dots of land, with only a dark gray ribbon of disturbed water marking its passage. A well used craft, low to the water, and roughly camouflaged to resemble a local motor driven dhow.

From the bridge of the surfaced submarine, a light flashed four quick times followed by a long flash and the two more quick ones. The motor boat returned the correct light signal. In a large graceful arc, the boat turned toward the American submarine.

A figure appeared on DALLAS's deck. It inched along carefully in the ankle deep water. The boat slowed as it came along the submarine's hull.

The boat stopped where the figure stood. A line from the craft's bow secured it to the submarine. The work was fast, the transfer quick. Her job complete, the line let go and the boat spurred ahead into the night.

Now, two figures slunk carefully along the hull. At the dry dock shelter, they disappeared inside. Immediately, DALLAS moved forward. As she turned for open water, geysers of vapor hissed from the vents. She settled slowly and melted into the black water.

Lapadnaya Lista
Russian Submarine Base

"Vadim," Danyankov said as he saluted.

Captain First Rank Vadim Lebedko returned the salute, and reached forward to shake his hand. "Valerik, how have you been?"

"I am well," Danyankov released his hand. "Tell me, have they chased you back to sea yet? Perhaps as next Captain?" he said as he nodded toward VEPR.

Lebedko lowered his head. "No, not yet."

Danyankov sensed something in the man's voice. "Then what brings you out of your office?"

Lebedko drew in a lungful of the cold Arctic air. "Your request for transfer has been denied."

"What?" Danyankov asked as his eyes blazed. "I..."

Lebedko raised his hand. "Valerik, this comes from the Defense Minister. I am to take you to the airfield. You leave for Moscow in thirty minutes."

Chapter Thirteen

TRUTHS TO BE TOLD

*"When one has one's hand full of truth
it is not always wise to open it."*
~French Proverb

Mystic, Connecticut
January 5th

In the early hours, a cold front pushed down from the Arctic. In the darkness, temperatures that struggled for the past few days to reach above freezing, fell again to sub-zero. As the frigid air continued toward the southeast, it collided headlong with air warmed by the Gulf Stream. The two masses of air danced around each other like boxers. The cold, dry air sought to bleed its opponent of energy as it collected moisture from its warmer foe. The warm air rose high as it slithered around the icy front. It reached as high as its own energy allowed before it pounced on the frenzied frigid air. The masses of air began to swirl, and the worst winter storm of the year was born.

Off the Grand Banks, a small, but well formed high-pressure system pushed the new storm on a southwesterly course, straight for the New England coast.

* * *

Grant McKinnon felt the wind pick up. He regretted not putting on a heavier coat. The cold seeped in a steady flow through his windbreaker.

A few more should do it, he thought as he balanced the seasoned oak logs in one arm. As he stood, he noticed the warm flicker of the fireplace through the frosted window.

McKinnon suddenly forgot about the cold, about the logs, about everything. Through the window, he could see Jennifer, her long red hair, the simple yet beautiful lines of her face.

Like the newly formed storm, forces in his brain battled for control. Hope and desire sparred with guilt and fear. Desire and hope had the upper hand now, as he saw the way she smiled. *I'm going to lose this battle.*

On the antique sofa, Jennifer finished the bedtime story as Misty's eyes grew heavy with sleep.

"Mommy, I like it here best of all," she said as she snuggled deeper in the quilt.

Jennifer smiled down at her daughter. "Why here?"

"It's always warm," the child replied with a deep yawn.

"Our house is warm," Jennifer said as she set the book of nighttime stories on the side table.

Misty's drooping eyes lifted. "It's a different warm. I feel good here."

Jennifer stroked her soft hair. "Me, too."

USS DALLAS SSN 700
The Red Sea

Four hundred feet below the busy sea-lane, DALLAS moved quietly southwest. With each turn of her screw, the tip of the Arabian Peninsula drew closer. By morning, the American submarine would pass unseen through the narrow Ta'izz Straights and into the Gulf of Aden.

In the wardroom, Commander Samuel Oliver welcomed his guest. "I hope you slept well, Captain," he smiled.

Captain Ellen Knotts looked around the tiny space. "God, I hate this already," she said as she sat in the chair closest to Oliver.

"You'll get used to it," He chuckled.

"I slept like the dead," Knotts said as she added a spoon of sugar to her coffee. "Of course, who wouldn't?"

"Rough trip?" Oliver asked.

Knotts sipped at her coffee. "I felt like a bag of cocaine being smuggled halfway around the planet."

The door of the wardroom opened. Lieutenant Commander Michael Warren, Commander of SEAL TEAM 4 stepped in.

"Hello, Captain," he smiled. "Mike Warren, CO of the SEALS." Warren extended his hand.

"Nice to meet you," Knotts replied.

"We met last night," Warren grinned.

"We did?" She asked puzzled.

"You remember the tall guy, face mask, pulling you out of the boat?"

"That was you?" She shook her head. "I was worried about being washed over the side."

"That would have been bad. That area is loaded with sea snakes and sharks."

"My mother would die," Knotts sighed.

"So," Oliver interrupted. "Why would they send you all the way here?"

Knotts set her cup on the blue table cover. "Three days ago, an Iranian submarine exploded off Bandar-E Abbas."

Commander Oliver's eyes widened. "Exploded?"

"Must have had a bad battery," Warren commented.

"No," Knotts rubbed her chin. "The Iranians said they were testing a new torpedo. They tested it all right; it turned around and killed the sub that shot it."

Both men sat back in their seats.

"I didn't know the Iranians had a new torpedo," Oliver shrugged.

"They don't," Knotts said.

"So what really killed the boat?" Warren asked.

Knotts ran her finger around the rim of the now empty coffee cup "That's why I'm here."

Oliver and Warren looked at each other.

Knotts turned the empty coffee cup over. "Your mission, Commander Oliver, is to get in close enough so Mr. Warren here can swim in and snap a few pictures of that sub."

"Wow," Commander Oliver joked.

"Not too tough, is it?" Knotts gave him a grin.

Warren leaned forward. "If Shootin' Sam here can get us within a mile, we can do it."

"What are the Iranians doing over the site?" Commander Oliver asked.

Knotts cocked her head. "That's what concerns us. They have yet to really dive the wreck."

"No guard ship?" Warren rubbed the stubble on his face. "They just said, 'Oh well, sucks to be them?'"

"Pretty much," Knotts replied. "So, do we go for it?"

DALLAS's Commander lifted his finger. "Just one question, Captain."

"Sure," Knotts answered.

"Why you? No offense, but you're not the field work type."

Knotts grimaced. "Wish the answer was more dramatic."

"We're listening," Warren said cautiously.

"I made the CNO look like a dork. So here I

am... being taught a lesson.”

“Big boys don't like playing with the girls, huh?” Oliver held her eyes.

“No, it's not that,” Knotts sighed. “I think risky ideas are supposed to be... suggested.”

“Ah, I see,” Commander Oliver nodded. “If Mr. Warren agrees, the mission's a go.”

Warren grinned and rubbed his hands together. “Let's do it.”

The Kremlin
Moscow, Russia

“Valerik,” the Minister of Defense greated him warmly, “please sit.” He pointed to the seat across from the great oak desk.

“Evelina will be worried.” Danyankov said as he took the seat offered. “I did not have time to tell her I was leaving.”

Vitenka lifted his hand. “Not to worry. I called my daughter and told her you would be with me.”

Danyankov wondered if she had told her father their news. “Did she say anything else?”

“No,” Vitenka answered cautiously. “She did sound tired. Is she well?”

“Of course!” Danyankov assured his father-in-law, as he pulled at the collar of his uniform.

The Defense Minister tapped his pen on the desk. “You are wondering why you are here, no doubt.”

“Yes, sir, and why my request for transfer

was denied."

Vitenka leaned forward until his elbows rested on the desk. "I was curious as to why you suddenly wanted a transfer." He studied his son-in-law's face. "We'll get to that matter another time."

"Sir, I have reasons, but I..."

"Valerik," Vitenka interrupted. "You know your father and I served many years together."

"I do," Danyankov replied. A tingle swept up the back of his head. He knew the feeling and it had served him well. *Here was trouble.*

"When you were small, Russia was in a bad shape. Our missiles were inferior, and too few in numbers. Had there been war with the United States, we could not have survived."

"I do not understand what this has to..."

"Please, hear me out," Vitenka interrupted softly. "It was thought then if war was inevitable, a first strike would be the only way to eliminate the American threat. We had no missiles to do the job. Our bombers had little chance of escaping American fighters," Vitenka adjusted himself in the large chair.

"In 1960, Khrushchev ordered our Chief Weapon designer, Sakharov, to develop a mine. A nuclear mine, with a yield of 50 kilotons."

Danyankov's mouth dropped open, "50 kilotons?"

"Quite an achievement," Vitenka nodded proudly. "A three stage weapon, in reality. We had yet to perfect our uranium purification, so we replaced the internal pit baffles with lead.

The lead in the second and third stages increased the yield by eliminating fast fission."

"I never knew about this," Danyankov murmured.

"No one did," Vitenka went on. "The warhead was fitted to a stainless steel shell. The rear half of one of our early electric torpedoes made it a fine weapon. Power for the arming circuit came from batteries charged by heat from deuterium of the warhead's natural nuclear decay."

"A weapon like that could last hundreds of years," Danyankov observed.

"Indeed," Vitenka nodded slowly. "All we needed was a means of detonation. That came when we developed a coded acoustic signal generator. By today's standards, it is a simple device. The warhead's fuse was coded to a set of three separate harmonics in a particular order. The sound generator detonator was built so that it could be plugged into the active sonar system of any submarine."

Danyankov sat fascinated. "Was this weapon ever deployed?"

The Minister drew in a deep breath. "Khrushchev was very fearful when Kennedy was elected. He ordered it deployed to... New York Harbor."

"No!" Danyankov sat bolt upright. The tingle now throbbed in the back of his neck.

"But there was one problem," Vitenka said as he lifted his index finger. "The Americans had learned from Pearl Harbor. They now guarded their coasts very well. Somehow we had to draw the American fleet away. By 1961, we had the plan in place."

"1961?" Danyankov muttered, scratching his jaw. "You mean—"

"The Cuban Missile Crisis was our decoy." Vitenka nodded.

Danyankov leaned forward, elbows on his thighs. "Minister, that decoy almost ended in nuclear war!"

"It went a bit out of hand," Vitenka nodded. "However, the mission to plant the device was a great success."

"One of our boats made it inside New York Harbor?" Danyankov pressed on.

Vitenka went silent, his weary eyes fixed on his son-in-law. But when he spoke again, his voice was filled with strength. "The Great Khrushchev asked for the best submarine commander in the fleet, and he got him."

"Which boat was able to get that far in?" Danyankov asked, dreading the answer.

Again, the Minister drew in a deep breath. "The K-14."

The tingle in Danyankov's head became an ice cap.

"Yes, Valerik, your father's." Vitenka's voice was filled with pride. "It was, up until that time and perhaps even now, the greatest achievement of a Sov... Russian submarine."

"And you were there?" Danyankov asked.

"I was. Officially as the navigator. Unofficially, I was the one assigned to arm the mine before its launch," Vitenka explained. "Your father would not have taken the mission had it not been for you. He told me this himself. He worried about an American strike on the base. At the time, it seemed inevitable."

"He never spoke of this," Danyankov stammered.

"We were sworn to secrecy!" Vitenka's eyes became focused on the past for a moment. "We were lucky to return from that mission. When the boat was tied to the pier, your mother brought you onboard. Your father was so happy. A son at last! He held you while I took a snapshot."

Danyankov thought of the gift Evelina had given him. A sudden deep sadness filled him. He had never really known his father, never understood.

"Why tell me this here, why now?" Danyankov asked weakly.

Vitenka got up and walked to the window. He peered out at the darkened parade ground. "The operation's code name was MAY HARVEST. I do not know why it was called that. The mine has lain there ever since."

Danyankov lurched in his seat, "Still there?"

Vitenka shrugged as he came back to his desk. "How could we ever retrieve it? You are here, Captain, because the file on MAY HARVEST containing the plans for the detonator are missing."

"Stolen?"

"Yes," Vitenka hissed.

"Who?"

Vitenka sat down. "Iran."

Danyankov's face twisted in surprise. "The Persians? They have no submarine that can reach America."

"True," Vitenka nodded as he settled in his chair.

"They have our Varshavyanka diesel boats.' Danyankov mused. "I have seen the training reports. They are less than expert in tactical application. I doubt one could make it into the Strait of Hormuz. The Americans would snap him up within a day."

Vitenka opened a desk drawer and removed the folder Admiral Onufriev had compiled. "I agree with all you have said, Captain, however, they have found a way." He handed the folder to his son-in-law.

As VEPR's Commander opened the coarse brown cover, Vitenka sat in silence, watching the Captain read.

"Do the Americans know about this?" Danyankov growled as he closed the folder.

"No, Valerik, and they cannot."

"But..."

"If the Americans knew of this, what do you expect they would do? For years they have wanted an excuse to attack Iran. *This* would be all they needed. Then how would we explain a 50 kiloton weapon buried under their noses all these years?"

"So, what do we do?" Danyankov scowled. "Is the weapon still operational?"

Vitenka looked toward the window. "I programmed it," he said sadly. "I can remember it as if it were last night. We launched it at 73 degrees, 55 minutes in 54 fathoms. We set the motor to run at 20 knots. It passed by Sandy Hook, then turned to course 330 over the Romer Shoal to the Bay Ridge Channel. Then, up to three meters for eight minutes. It then turned to course 060 for three more minutes before a final course of 358 for two minutes. There, it sank to the bottom."

Danyankov felt his throat go dry. "Where is that?"

"The last place the Americans would look," Vitenka lowered his head.

"Where?" Danyankov asked again.

Zivon Vitenka's old eyes looked up. "At the base of Ellis Island."

Danyankov's eyes went wide. He fought to form words. "A 50 kiloton blast there would destroy New York. Incinerate millions of people." He tried to swallow. "More when the tidal wave obliterated the New Jersey shore."

"I know," Vitenka whispered. "I planned it that way."

"If the Persians do detonate the mine, it will take only hours for the Americans to determine where it was detonated and then where the weapon came from. They know terrorists are unlikely to attack from the sea..."

Vitenka finished the thought, "And that would leave them with only one conclusion."

For the first time in his long career, Valerik

Danyankov felt fear slip like a cold knife along his spine. "They will retaliate," he managed.

The air in the Minister's office seemed to grow colder, the lights dimmer. Vitenka folded his hands on the desk. "Of course, the Americans will retaliate, and then we will shoot our rockets at them. Just what the Iranians want!"

"Madmen," Danyankov hissed.

"Who?" asked Vitenka. "Who is more insane, us, the Americans or the Iranians?"

"All of us." Danyankov thought of how happy he had been only hours before. He thought of Evelina. He could see her smile as she went about her chores. In his mind's eye, he saw his wife in her favorite dress, in her arms their son lay asleep... and he saw the entire apartment evaporate in a sudden burst of white-hot light as an American ICBM detonated over the base. In an instant, they were gone. Hopelessness now curled around his mind. "What can we do?"

"Khrushchev asked for the best submarine commander in the fleet to carry out that mission. Now I ask for the best to find and destroy the Iranian submarine before it gets to the American coast."

Danyankov felt the new fear slither around to his ribs. *Had my father felt the same?* More questions slammed into his head. *What if I can't find the Persian? What if the Americans find me?* A KILO and an AKULA off their coast, the Americans would go out of their minds. He thought of the new VIRGINIA Class American submarines based out of New London.

Danyankov felt like weeping as he looked up at the ornate ceiling. *It is as if someone cruel has written my life for me.*

He suddenly felt the need to tell his father-in-law about the baby. *Would that change his mind?*

Danyankov needed no modesty. He was the best the Russian navy had. *What if Vitenka sent someone else? Who would it be? Alekseev, K-461 VOLK? No, she had been used for spare parts in the Pacific boats.*

Swiftly, he reviewed all the boats they had, and still came up with only one answer. K-157 VEPR. Still, a small voice whispered in his mind, *What if you fail?* The stakes this time were far too high for arrogance to ignore. "It will be hard to break into the Atlantic," he said quietly.

Vitenka's voice now sounded tired and old, "I leave the details to you."

"How long until the tanker is in a position for intercept?"

"We estimate seven days, perhaps less," Vitenka replied.

"If I could sink the tanker and the submarine in deep water..." Danyankov said, mostly to himself.

"Tonight, you will stay with me," Vitenka announced, getting to his feet. "In the morning, you fly back to your command. You will sail the day after."

"It will take time to provision," Danyankov muttered.

"That is already being done."

Danyankov sighed as the weight of the task settled over him. "I would like to go into the city. I have not seen Moscow in years."

"Of course," Vitenka replied. "Pick up something nice for my daughter."

Chapter Fourteen

LONG DISTANCE

*"Somehow our devils
are never quite what we expect
when we meet them face to face."*
~Nelson DeMille

Aboard the Iranian Oil Tanker
Behzad Nabavi
January 6th

Feroz was groggy and weak. He looked down in the pale, sickly light to the puddle of sweat around his feet. Each breath was an effort as his lungs protested the vile toxic atmosphere.

From the tiny compartment near the hatch, SIMCER's commander lifted the phone handset from its cradle and dialed the tanker's bridge.

"What is our position?" He asked weakly.

"10 kilometers off Aden," a voice replied through static.

Feroz looked at the hatch. "Is it dark?"

"Yes, sir, sunset was an hour ago."

Feroz hooked the handset back in the cradle. He stumbled to the edge of the deck. "Start the pumps," he shouted over the side.

Below him, men, stripped to their waists, moved like the walking dead, their steps slow and labored, uncertain. Feroz noticed the shadowy outline of the men's ribs. He wondered how many would make it to the target alive. Not that it mattered. He did, however, hope enough survived to operate SIMCER.

The whine of the pumps began. Feroz waited until all seven machines were operational before he activated the hatch mechanism. At once, the putrid dank air rushed past him as it escaped into the atmosphere.

Immediately, water sloshed in below until it covered the first deck. Here the massive pumps managed to keep the level at bay. However, their operation caused the temperature in the shell to climb.

Five minutes later, Feroz reversed the hydraulic actuator and the hatch clamped shut. He picked up the phone. "Pump in air now," he barked.

The rumble of a compressor echoed through the steel walls. Feroz cleared his ears as pressure in the shell rose.

USS DALLAS SSN 700
30 Miles off Aden

The Control Room was black as Commander Oliver stepped to the periscope stand. Newly qualified Officer of the Deck, Lieutenant Anton Fischer, called Oliver to the plot table.

"What's the problem, Mr. Fisher?"

"Sir, the ship is making preparations to come to periscope depth. We cleared our baffles to the south. When I came back to base course, sonar picked up a strange surface contact."

"Sonar, Conn, what did you find, Chief?" Oliver asked over the open microphone.

"Conn, Sonar," a voice replied. "We hold Sierra-67 on passive broadband tracker 2. Contact now bears 289, Range by bottom bounce 8,000 yards on the left drawing left. Contact is a deep merchant making 7-0 turns on two five bladed screws."

"What's so strange?" Oliver asked

"Conn, Sonar, we hold unusual flow noises from the contact. We have also picked up transients from the contact."

"Can you classify?"

There was a pause, "Conn, Sonar, aye. Believe the transients to be high discharge pumps. We now hold a machinery noise, believed to be a compressor."

"Interesting," Oliver shrugged.

"I thought maybe the tanker might be taking water and in trouble," Fischer explained.

"Good call," Oliver said. "Lets' go up and take a peak. If he's in trouble, we'll send a message and get him some assistance."

Moscow, Russia

Danyankov stepped slowly along the sidewalk. Moscow had changed since his last visit. More lights, more shops. A large glowing neon sign caught his eye. *How did an American colonel get permission to sell chicken here?*

He noticed more cars. More people about who were smiling. More couples. More babies. *If they only knew.*

He stopped under a lamppost plastered with tattered posters and flyers offering every service from car repair to dance club tickets. *If this was all they had to worry about, they would be grateful.*

A small corner shop caught Danyankov's eye. He looked in the window at an assortment of tiny bells, formed from delicate cut crystal. The facets caught the light just right and seemed to explode into a lovely rainbow. He remembered the porcelain bells on the shelf of their apartment. *At least it will be something.*

Inside, the shop was warm and smelled of eucalyptus. Items from every region of Russia and around the world lined shelves and filled glass display cases.

The large woman behind the counter smiled at Danyankov.

"Help you, Captain?"

"Yes," he smiled back. "The bells?"

"Ah," she nodded as she waddled from her stool to the case. "From America." She opened the case and carefully handed one to Danyankov. "Very hard to get," she added. "They come from Connecticut."

Danyankov turned the tiny bell in his hand. "Connecticut?"

"They have a very famous crystal factory there," she nodded. "I am told they also make submarines there."

Her words triggered his brain. *McKinnon.*

"Excuse me?" The sales lady frowned.

He had not realized he had spoken. "Just thinking aloud," he said as he handed back the bell. "I will take it."

"Very good choice, Captain," she cooed as her massive hands pulled tissue paper from a hidden roll under the cabinet.

"Do you have a box?" He asked. "I fly tomorrow."

Skillfully, she wrapped the bell in dull pink tissue paper, and settled the bundle into a pretty blue cardboard box. "There."

McKinnon's name again came to him. He respected the American and begrudgingly admitted only to himself that the American Captain was every bit as skilled as he was. Perhaps more.

The woman carried the box over to the register. Danyankov paid her and pocketed the small parcel.

"Safe journey, Captain!" She called as he stepped out into the cold street.

Would McKinnon do it? Danyankov's mind weighed the risks. The one factor that trumped all else was Evelina and the baby.

Mystic, Connecticut

"Is she asleep?" McKinnon asked softly.

Jennifer nodded.

"The weatherman was right for once," McKinnon sighed.

Jennifer slowly moved Misty to the end of the plush sofa. She tucked the quilt up under the child's chin. "I can hear the ice on the window," she murmured.

A gust of wind moaned as it blew around the old house. The warm lights of the antique chandelier flickered, then blinked out.

"There goes the power!" McKinnon said as he looked at the now dark bulbs.

"We'll freeze," Jennifer said with some alarm. "I should try to get home."

McKinnon smiled. "Don't think you should try that. Remember what happened the time you drove in the snow?"

"But with no heat..."

"Don't worry," McKinnon got to his feet. "Every room has a fireplace, and there's enough wood to last all winter."

A look came over Jennifer's face. "Every

room?" She murmured.

"Every one," McKinnon answered innocently.

Jennifer stood and stepped slowly to him. Her slender arms wrapped around his shoulders as her lips pressed against his. "Does that include your bedroom?"

Moscow, Russia

Hours ticked by as if each minute held its breath. Valerik Danyankov's tired, heavy eyes refused the blessed sleep he needed. His exhausted body tossed under the covers, his mind crowded with questions it could not answer. Every option, every tactic in his inventory of experience was useless. *How can I break out without being seen?* He kept asking.

The British and Americans both announced they no longer used SOSUS, the string of underwater listening devices planted decades ago on the sea floor for the sole purpose of locating all of Russia's submarines.

What if they detect me? A second-generation AKULA suddenly appearing out of home waters would surely invite a scramble of the usual hostile submarines and surface ships. Perhaps even Norwegian, and German.

Danyankov's mind returned repeatedly to his only option, his one hope. Grant McKinnon.

USS DALLAS SSN 700

The American submarine leveled 60 feet beneath the three-foot swells that rolled gently atop the night sea. "Put me on the bearing," Commander Oliver ordered.

"Contact now bears 320," Fire Control reported.

Oliver swung the scope left. "There she is," he said as the tanker's dark hull filled the image-intensified optics. "Target shows normal lights. She's moving at speed."

"Conn, Sonar, machinery noises have stopped."

"Sonar, Conn, aye," Oliver acknowledged. "Well, gentlemen, looks like she's doing just fine. Quartermaster, make a log entry in case this comes back on us."

Lapadnaya Lista
Russian Submarine Base

Only a long ribbon of deep purple set against the hills marked Arctic winter noon time.

As Valerik Danyankov stepped down from the plane, his boots crunched loudly in the fresh snow. Three meters away a car waited for him. A junior officer who Danyankov didn't know opened the door of the shabby sedan.

"Home, sir?" The officer asked as he climbed behind the wheel.

"No," Danyankov huffed. "Headquarters."

Mystic, Connecticut

The wind still moaned in the darkness, as Grant McKinnon awoke. Jennifer, soft and warm, lay next to him, the outline of her body under the down-filled quilt silhouetted in the final glow of the fire's dying embers. His mind searched for the guilt that had tugged at him ever since she'd come into his life. He tried hard to find it, almost wanted it.

He leaned over, wrapped his arm around her. The smell of her hair, the softness of her bare skin allowed only one emotion. A wave of relief passed through him, as if something lifted him up, something that made him smile.

Carefully, he got out of bed and stepped to the door. The old wood-plank floor was cold under his feet. The air, though, was warm. He clicked the light switch in the bathroom. The antique fixture came on. *Power's back.* He showered quickly, then dressed.

He trod gently down the stairs into the kitchen. He smiled as he looked out the frosted window where the snow was still swirling in a white mist.

For a brief second, he thought of not going to the base. *I have to.* He quietly slid the empty carafe into the coffee maker. *She's up there,* another part of his mind teased.

"I have to think," he whispered aloud. As he waited for the coffee to brew, he tried to busy his mind with the day's agenda. Navigator scheduled to hold officer training at 0900. Then meet with the Repair Officer about new cells for the oxygen generator.

Soon, the aroma of coffee filled the old kitchen. It seemed he'd never known such a glad smell, even though he'd brewed it for years in the same machine. *How different life seemed today.* He eased open the 100-year old door to the pantry, careful to avoid the usual squeak from its ancient hinges. From a shelf, he retrieved a brown bag and took out one of Mystic Bakery's finest, fresh bagels.

As it toasted and the coffee dripped, McKinnon took stock of all that had happened, and could only wonder at what came next. So much in so little time. *Time,* he thought as he removed the bagel from the toaster oven. *Wait too long, and your life's over. Don't wait and you might scare her off.* He rolled his shoulders as he bit into the warm tasty bread. *You big dope, just enjoy what you have now!*

Breakfast done, he tidied up. As he reached for his coat, the telephone let out its low electronic buzz. He snatched the receiver from the wall, hoping he'd picked up before the phone next to his bed had rung. "Hello," he growled a bit irritated. Then he froze. "Danyankov?"

Chapter Fifteen

PIRATES

*"Promise only what you can deliver.
Then deliver more than you promise."*
~Author Unknown

USS DALLAS SSN 700
16 Miles off the Iranian Naval Base
Bandar-E Abbas
January 7th

She made good time in the cooler waters of the deep ocean. With no real threat, either surfaced or submerged, Commander Oliver drove DALLAS ahead at flank speed.

Once in the Gulf of Oman, DALLAS slowed. Traffic in the now narrow water increased from one lonely ship to 34 contacts. Oliver picked his way through freighters, tankers, numerous dhows and other vessels whose purpose was known only to those who sailed them.

As the sun sliced through the last of night, DALLAS moved north. Out of the traffic and noise of the busy waterway, the jumble of sonar contacts faded astern. After a few slow miles, the seabed rose up on a gentle angle. The American submarine followed the contour until it leveled off on a vast plain with only 400 feet of clear water.

Just before noon, DALLAS entered the shallow water within site of the main Iranian naval base.

"We're here," Commander Oliver whispered. He nudged the scope around as his trained eye searched for threats.

Captain Knotts stood out of the way near the BSY-2 Fire Control weapon monitor panel. "What's out there?"

With his eyes locked to the periscope, Oliver pointed to a small monitor over the target plot. "Very strange," he noted. "Don't see a thing."

Lieutenant Commander Michael Warren also stood in the Control Room. "If we lost a boat, the place would be locked down."

"Don't I know it!" Oliver muttered. "Sonar, you hold any transients?"

"Conn, Sonar, no," a hushed voice replied.

Oliver handed the scope to Warren. "ESM Conn, do you hold any contacts?"

At the tip of DALLAS's number two periscope, a radar detector sniffed the air for electronic pulses. Computers received, analyzed, then classified the information and provided the operator a liquid crystal display of the results.

"Conn, ESM, holds one ESM contact designate Romeo 1. Classified as TIN SHIELD; land based air defense radar. Romeo 1 is in low PRF mode. This contact is no detection threat. Signal strength three."

"Does this make sense to you?" Oliver whispered to the SEAL.

"None," Warren shrugged. "Sure is interesting though."

Oliver leaned over the chart. His finger traced a line along his intended route. "We'll creep in nice and slow. If we have no activity by 1500, we'll get your boys out for a swim."

Naval Submarine Base
Groton, Connecticut

Grant McKinnon's mind processed a faint voice that entered his ear. The image of a mushroom cloud visible just beyond New London's bleak skyline faded as the faint voice came again.

"Skipper?" The voice asked through the whistle of the wind. "Skipper, you okay?"

Half dazed, McKinnon turned. Chief of the Boat, Danny Norse, his face reddened by the stinging ice, shivered.

"COB?" McKinnon shrugged.

"You're gonna freeze out here," Norse's teeth chattered.

"COB," McKinnon blinked. "I want an Officer

Call in the wardroom in fifteen minutes.

"Something up?" Norse asked as both men trudged through the ankle-deep slush.

McKinnon's eyes told the 24-year submarine veteran all he needed to know.

Lapadnaya Lista
Russian Submarine Base

"This is more than a training mission, isn't it?" Evelina frowned.

Valerik Danyankov knew his wife's experience of her father's days at sea. Her voice questioned, but her eyes knew the answer. He searched his limited vocabulary for a case like this.

"Don't worry," he forced a smile. "Remember who you married." Instantly, he knew how wrong that must sound.

"I know precisely who I married," she wiped away the tears streaking down her cheeks. "This is why I worry. If my father called you to Moscow, it must be very bad."

Danyankov's mind drifted to his own father. *What would he have said?* The Commanding Officer of the most feared Russian submarine in the Northern Fleet struggled for words.

"I know our ships do not go to sea unless there is trouble. You told me that. Now suddenly, you are going to sea," she laid her head on his chest. "Is it that bad?"

Again, he found himself checkmated. He

could not lie to her, nor could he tell her the truth.

For a brief instant, Danyankov thought of sending her off on the weekly supply train. If he failed to find the Iranian submarine, chances were very good Lapadnaya Lista would be little more than a glowing pile of molten radioactive limestone and granite. *Where would she go?* He looked into her puffy red eyes. *If the missiles come, there is no place to hide.*

Thankfully, she changed the subject on her own. "Did you tell my father about the baby?"

"No," he answered, glad to be truthful. Glad he had not told him. He gently stroked his wife's hair with his fingers. "You keep it a secret until I get back. We will both fly to Moscow and see the look on his face."

She managed a smile. "Promise you will be back."

Aboard the Iranian Oil Tanker
Behzad Nabavi

In the night, *Behzad Nabavi* passed easily through the Suez Canal. By dawn, the cooler waters of the Mediterranean lapped the tanker's 860 foot hull. In the shell, the temperature dropped 22 degrees in as many hours.

Feroz had the SIMCER's batteries checked. Although motionless, some of the submarine's systems relied on them. The snake-like power umbilical provided most of what it needed, but not enough to keep a full charge. Feroz knew he would eventually have to start SIMCER's diesels to give the KILO's batteries a full charge.

Even with the temperature in the shell down to an almost bearable range, other problems now showed up. The heat and humidity worked quickly to rot food not in cans. And those were not always reliable. Pressure from the open hatch and the compressor had already ruptured many.

Of the three hastily welded 2500-liter steel tanks of drinking water, one leaked from a poor weld, another tasted of pesticide, or kerosene. The last tank contained a briny solution that emitted the stench of rotten eggs.

Oil, spoiled food, garbage, and human waste collected in a putrid pool under the submarine's stern. He had thought the forward motion of the old tanker would carry the mass of floating waste out into the ocean. However, the bulbous bow of the submarine that protruded just under the line of the tanker's keel caused a low pressure area as the water flowed in and around the KILO's hull.

At the tapered stern, the pressure reduced further and locked the filth inside. The festering brown-green lake swirled and bubbled. Fumes rose in a noxious vapor to the roof of the shell. With nowhere to escape, the vapor condensed, and fluid dripped down over man and machine.

Sickness came soon. From foul water, toxic air, rotted food, heat, and the constant change in pressure. Men hacked and coughed. Many suffered painful cramps, and diarrhea. Scratches and minor injuries developed infection, as the men's gaunt bodies lost all ability to fight off any bacteria.

Feroz, himself weak from coughing and diarrhea, looked over the flimsy rail of the shell's third level. Below him, those of the crew that could, accomplished or attempted their assigned tasks in slow motion.

For the past two nights, SIMCER's Captain kept to himself in the cramped sheet metal compartment at the shell's highest level. He knew men in these conditions were liable to resort to any means to regain their comfort. Each day, he oiled the 9mm automatic pistol he carried in a now slimy leather holster.

"Pirates!" Feroz rasped into the filthy air.

Chapter Sixteen

ANSWERS AND QUESTIONS

*"No problem can withstand
the assault of sustained thinking."*
~Voltaire

USS DALLAS SSN 700
5 Miles from Bandar-E Abbas

DALLAS hovered motionless in the warm water off the Iranian naval base. The Diving Officer had perfectly positioned every ounce of water in the submarine's trim tanks. With only 40 feet above her sail and 75 feet under the keel, there was no margin for error.

"Conn, Sonar," a frantic voice called over the 27MC. "Twin diesel lines just started. Bearing 278. Designate Sierra-22. We hold an up doppler shift. Range decreasing. Closest point of approach will be in three minutes, bearing 323 range 100 yards."

"Damn!" Commander Oliver swore as he spun the periscope toward the sudden noise. "There it is," he announced. "Fire Control match bearings."

"Solution set," the Fire Control operator said. "Recommend high speed run to enable."

"Set high speed run to enable," Oliver barked. In one motion, DALLAS's Captain slapped the handles of the scope into their stowed position. "Down scope."

Sitting wide-eyed on a bench near the BPS-15 Radar, Knotts did not understand all the terminology, but she understood enough to cause beads of sweat to appear just blow the line of her dark blonde hair.

"Captain..."

"Not now," Oliver snapped.

"Conn, Sonar, constant bearing rate from Sierra-22, no change in speed," Sonar reported.

"Nasty little patrol boat," Oliver said as he rubbed his neck.

The Petty Officer at the Fire Control plot looked up from his digital map. "Captain Sierra-22 is at minimum engagement range."

"Very well, plot," Oliver responded with little concern in his voice. "Okay, folks, we have a bad guy going to pass right over us."

Knotts looked around her. Not a man moved or even twitched.

"Time to rendezvous?" Oliver whispered.

"Eight minutes," the Navigator replied.

From outside the hull, a faint low whine

disturbed the silence. At first, it sounded like an electric fan. Then grew louder until it sounded like a distant lawnmower.

"How you holding up?" Oliver asked.

"I'll never leave my desk again," Knotts managed through clenched teeth. "I will get a bumper sticker that says I LOVE MY DESK."

"Don't worry, Captain," Oliver laughed softly. "That guy just happens to be in our part of the ocean."

The noise now grew until it sounded as if a freight train was only inches from their heads. Knotts instinctively ducked her head.

The noise of the patrol boat's twin diesels reached a crescendo. Books, battle lanterns, pens and pencils in DALLAS's Control Room vibrated slightly as pressure of the sound waves entered the hull. Then, as quickly has it had begun, the vibration ceased.

Knotts lifted her head as the noise faded off the American submarine's port side.

"See, Captain," Oliver said out of the side of his mouth. "No clue we're here."

Knott's chest heaved as her nerve-wracked body drew in the cool air. "What if they had?"

Oliver shrugged. "Just be happy they didn't."

"Swimmers in the dock," the sound powered phone operator announced.

Oliver checked his watch. "Boys are home early."

Aboard the Iranian Oil Tanker
Behzad Nabavi
200 Miles South of Yíthion, Greece

The battery charge was completed soon after the last rays of the sun faded.

For Feroz and his crew, the two hours of SIMCER's diesels was enough. A makeshift sleeve clamped over the KILO's snorkel mast, now provided outside air for the oxygen-hungry engines. Constructed of light flexible sheets of rolled aluminum, the sleeve connected the mast to a vent valve installed in the shell's roof.

In theory, the valve would open and shut depending on the submarine's needs. What no one had thought of was the pressure in the shell. As the engine started, the flexible sleeve all but collapsed. The diesels ran rough as the required air was choked off and on. When the diesels needed more air, vacuum breakers in the submarine's air manifold opened and drew it in from the interior of the shell.

Men moaned and covered their ears with their hands as the changes in pressure assaulted eardrums. Then as the air in the shell was sucked out, the sea rushed in. The massive pumps fought the rising water level until the compressor could again raise atmospheric pressure. The tug-of-war between the air and sea seemed to last for an eternity. Finally, Feroz had to order the engines secured.

The only benefit, other than fresh power

stored in the KILO's batteries, was that the entire foul atmosphere of the steel cavern had been replaced by sweet-tasting cool air from the European continent.

As *Behzad Nabavi* continued on her course, cool clean Mediterranean water began to dissipate built-up heat as it leeched out of the steel plates.

In the shell, the results were immediate. The hazy fog evaporated. Lights glowed brighter in the clear air. Men stirred and moved more readily. Lungs could breathe again, heads cleared, and appetites more or less returned.

USS DALLAS SSN 700

Lieutenant Commander Mike Warren stepped down from the escape trunk lower hatch, his hair and face dripped with the brine of the Persian Gulf. "We need to talk," he huffed as another SEAL removed the closed circuit re-breather from his back.

"Everyone okay?" Commander Oliver asked as Warren peeled the top of his wetsuit down, and nodded as he was handed a cup of ice water. He drank all of it. "That was no submarine."

"What?" Knotts asked.

Warren turned to another returning SEALS. "Joe, get that camera disk processed, pronto."

"What about the sub?" Knotts asked again.

Warren shook his head. "Don't know what

these guys are up to, but what we found wasn't a sub. The metal was rusted as if it had been down there for years. We couldn't find one thing that even looked like it belonged on a submarine."

"Maybe the blast..." Knotts started.

"Captain," Warren cut her off. "A torpedo blast leaves more than that. There's just not enough metal... or debris."

"I've got a bad feeling about this," Oliver muttered.

"We did find a body," Warren said.

"Human?" Knotts asked.

"Oh yeah, brought him back too. Need to get him on ice for our people in Bahrain."

Knotts paled. "Why did you do that?"

Warren wrapped a dry towel around his neck. "The guy's almost without a scratch. Not one wound that matches any blast damage." Warren looked at Commander Oliver. "Something's up, sir."

USS MIAMI SSN 755
Naval Submarine Base
Groton, Connecticut

"What would prevent us from getting underway?" McKinnon asked the gathered officers.

"I have an inspection of the reduction gears scheduled for next week," the Engineer replied.

"I've got an upgrade to Fire Control coming

this weekend, plus optical tube alignment," the Weapons Officer added.

"Cancel everything," McKinnon said. "We need to be ready for sea at an hour's notice."

"What's going on?" The Navigator asked.

"I need you in my stateroom when we're done here," McKinnon nodded to him.

"I'll need to do a stores load," the Supply Officer announced.

"Get the request submitted today and schedule it for tomorrow."

McKinnon had done exactly what he had hoped not to. He looked at the faces and knew he had just caused a quiet panic. He could see the gears turning in minds of the smartest officers the country produced.

"Listen, fellas," he sighed. "I need you all at the ready. Can't give you details. I want two duty sections onboard until I say otherwise. That's all for now."

K-157 VEPR
Lapadnaya Lista
Russian Submarine Base

"Captain," the Radio Officer said softly, "here are the coordinates you asked for."

Commander Danyankov read the print out. "A new message will arrive every six hours. You are to bring it directly to me."

"Yes, sir," the officer replied.

"Go," Danyankov ordered. When the door

shut, he read the message again. *Off Greece. Three days to open sea.* He calculated it in his head. *If I can get out undetected, I can catch her mid-Atlantic.*

Another rap at his door interrupted his thoughts. "Come in," he growled.

Lieutenant Shurgatov stepped in. "Captain, we have a problem with the radio direction finder lift hoist."

"Fix it," Danyankov replied.

"Parts, sir," Shurgatov countered. "There are no spares."

"Is our sister ship DRAKON still in port?"

"Yes, Captain."

"Take what you need from her," Danyankov barked. "Use your head, Lieutenant!"

"But, Captain Nikitin will protest," Shurgatov stepped back as his Captain's eyes narrowed and his lip curled.

"Go get what we need," Danyankov hissed. "Trust me, by the time you get there, Captain Nikitin will be unbolting DRAKON's hoist himself."

"Captain?" Shurgatov dared to ask, "Are we going to sea?"

"Get the hoist fixed!"

Chapter Seventeen

HIGH STAKES POKER

*"A gambler is nothing but a man
who makes his living out of hope."*
~William Bolitho

Office of the Commander
Submarine Group Six
Naval Submarine Base
Groton, Connecticut

"I think we'll have to shut the base down," Admiral Tarrent said as he strode into his office. He kicked a layer of snow and ice from his shoes. "Weatherman says at least another 15 hours of this stuff."

"The lower base is a mess," Grant McKinnon added.

Tarrent shook the thin layer of snow from his coat. "Captain Farmer said you needed to see me. Must be important for you to drive up that hill," He said hanging hisheavy black coat over the heat register.

"It is," McKinnon sighed.

"Well?"

"I need to get to sea," McKinnon said softly.

"Right now?" The Admiral moved to his desk. "Why?"

McKinnon's mind swarmed with words but none made any sense. "I'd like to do some shallow water operations. You know, keep the boys in shape." *It was the truth*, McKinnon told himself. *Play these cards sparingly.*

Tarrent plopped himself heavily in his worn leather chair. "From your patrol report, you and your boys did just fine."

"Always room for improvement," McKinnon added with a forced smile.

"Budget's tight this month, Commander. I've got two boats headed to the Med, one South on drug ops and another North for NATO games."

"I could run rabbit for the Med boats," McKinnon offered. "Go a couple weeks early, really give 'em some effective shallow water training."

"A couple of weeks?" Tarrent snorted. "Did you hear what I just said? We're tight on cash."

McKinnon found himself frustrated. "Burke, just a few days."

Tarrent could read a man's face "Okay, Grant, what's going on?"

"I... can't say," McKinnon said quietly. "But I have to put to sea within three days."

Tarrent rested his elbows on the desk. "You know something I don't?"

"Yes, sir," McKinnon responded.

"What?" Tarrent smiled. "Another U-boat risen from its grave?"

McKinnon felt the color drain from his face. "Burke, this is worse than that U-boat trapped under the ice cap."

"That almost started a war, son." Tarrent growled. "What could be worse?"

"Sir, I..."

"I can tell you what would be worse," Tarrent said as he lifted a finger in the air and stabbed it at McKinnon. "Last week the Iranians lost a KILO."

"I heard," McKinnon said.

"Didn't really lose it. All a damned show. DALLAS went in yesterday and found no submarine wreckage."

"You think it slipped out?" McKinnon asked, hopefully.

"Of course it did!" Tarrent snorted and bumped a clenched fist on his desk. "The Secretary of Defense is sure the thing's out there after one of our carriers." He paused pinning McKinnon with his eyes. "What's on your mind?"

"The Iranians may be crazy, but not stupid. Maybe they found a way to..." McKinnon fought to keep from speaking what he knew. " What... what do you think they're doing?"

"Wish I knew," Tarrent grimaced. "But there

are pieces to this puzzle that are starting to fit. An Iranian submarine on the loose and you, with company at home, suddenly wanting to go to sea."

"I don't see how you make those particular pieces fit," McKinnon hedged.

"Come on, Grant! There's one thing you don't understand," Tarrent said as his eyes narrowed. "This is all a big game."

"What?" McKinnon asked.

"Like high stakes poker. Everyone already has the cards they're dealt."

"Please explain," McKinnon murmured.

"Remember Admiral Vitenka?" Tarrent tilted his head and raised his eyebrows, like a teacher waiting for a dull student's answer.

"Of course, he's now the Russian Minister of Defense."

"Called the Chairman of the Joint Chiefs. Didn't give us much to go on, but he thinks the Iranians are up to no good on our side of The Pond." Tarrent pinned McKinnon with his eyes. "And then here you come, suddenly wanting to go to sea."

"So, how do you figure I fit in?"

"Captain Danyankov's Vitenka's son-in-law. The two of you were... friendly foes, the last time I heard. Figure if it was this important, he'd make contact with you."

"What are you going to do?" McKinnon asked.

"Me?" Tarrent snorted a laugh. "Lesson two.

It's an election year, son. What do you think's going to happen if the politicians got wind of this?"

McKinnon's head began to throb. "Don't know, sir."

"Someone would leak it. Both parties need something to impress the press and the voters. The Democrats would blow this news sky high. The Military would have its hands tied tight. Information sources would be sieves. We might even lose a lot of funding."

"But…"

"Let me finish," Tarrent said with a wave of his hand. "Our biggest fear would be appeasement. A lot of folks are of the mind that if we just give Iran and North Korea, and a few others what they want, the world would be one big happy family."

"What about the President?"

Tarrent ran his hand through his thin gray hair. "The man never spent a day in uniform. For that matter, neither has any of his Cabinet." He glowered up at McKinnon. "Certain problems we have to handle ourselves. Easier to get forgiveness than permission, you know."

"Is that legal?" McKinnon asked feebly.

"Grant, you and I are tools. We are the hammer. The hammer does not decide which nail to hit."

McKinnon shook his head, "I don't like this."

"Don't be a hypocrite!" Tarrent snapped.

"You came in here to get a few days at sea. Were you about to tell me why?"

McKinnon looked down at his hands. *His Commanding Officer was right.*

"Now, Captain," Tarrent rumbled, "Get your boat ready for sea."

As he got to his feet, Grant McKinnon wondered just how much the Admiral already knew. As the door closed behind him, he felt the hunter in him stir.

Chapter Eighteen

STORM

"Every mile is two in winter."
~George Herbert

Aboard the Iranian Oil Tanker
Behzad Nabavi
January 10th

Clear of the Gibraltar Strait, the tanker eased into the Atlantic.

As shades of blue turned dark lavender, those on the bridge noticed an easterly shift in the slight wind. The tanker's navigator, with little experience outside the confined waters of the Persian Gulf, paid little attention to the barometer's needle as it fell.

Night came early, as high cumulonimbus formations choked what remained of daylight into darkness. Gusts slapped at the plodding tanker like unseen hands out of the black sky.

Lines rigged along the hull, shrieked and moaned as the gusts became a steady gale.

The sea also protested. Driven by 30-knot drafts, the ocean's surface rose in mounds which peaked and broke, only to form even larger swells.

Headlong the *Behzad Nabavi* drove into the gale. A normal ship of her size would take such a storm as little more than a nuisance. *Behzad Nabavi*, however, was no longer anything near normal.

Towers of angry water whipped white by the collision of sea and steel, rose high over the tanker's bow before gravity dragged them down in sheets of foam and spew.

Behzad Nabavi rode well in the sea. She met the 15-foot swells head on, her great bulk and length rolled easily over the crests of the larger waves, while her sheer tonnage smashed small rollers into mist.

Though the rise and fall of the great blunted nose of the tanker was only a few feet, to those in the bow, it felt as if the world dropped from under them only to have it hurtle back up.

Weakened men clung like rats to whatever would hold them. Those who lost their grip on the slippery rail, fell head first to the unyielding deck or backwards into the rusted plating. All became seasick. The sound of retching echoed in the quiet before the crash of the next wave.

As the size of the waves increased, Commander Feroz noticed SIMCER shifting slightly to port. He shouted to the Engineer over the thunder of water slamming down on the top of the shell.

When the bow rose, the small submarine lurched back to starboard. Twice the Engineer fell to the steel deck as he clambered over to the support arm.

Now, the tanker's bow lifted higher. Steel began to groan as the strain on the support arms doubled.

Feroz descended the flimsy ladder as it shook and vibrated. Curtains of water erupted from the KILO's side as the tanker rose and fell. Feroz crawled through the flood toward the Engineer.

Another sheet of water erupted as Feroz inched to where the Engineer held desperately to the swivel socket of the support arm.

"What is the problem?" Feroz bellowed over the roar of the furious water.

The nearly drowned Engineer pointed to the pin that mated the tanker to the submarine. "The hole has stretched," he yelled as water crashed onto steel. "A crack. At the base," he sputtered as another blanket of the cold Atlantic washed over them. "The pin will fall out if we don't weld it back."

"Rig the leads," Feroz screamed.

Men staggered and fell as soaked hands lost their grips. Seasick, nearly starved crewmen moved like phantoms in the knee-deep water as they made their way to the thin welding leads snaking from the SIMCER's squat sail.

The tanker's bow kept rising higher, and the 2,500-ton KILO swung with each rise and fall. Shrieking steel protested, as pressure from the waves and the weight of the submarine pressed down.

Feroz saw the white angry water reach for him, screaming like something evil. He reached for the support arm just as the water lashed with a vile hiss over him and the Engineer.

When the water receded, gurgling back into the sea, Feroz shook the stinging salt water from his eyes and saw he was alone.

A movement next to the KILO's side caught his eye. A bloodied hand reached up from the roiling water, its fingers opened wide in desperation. A smaller wave slapped along the KILO's limber holes toward the hand. The grinding hiss shuddered down the submarine's side as if the sea laughed. Feroz watched as the small wave suddenly reared up and fell over the hand. Again, the water drained away and the hand was gone.

Feroz grabbed at the arc welder leads as they whipped about in the swirls of water.

Suddenly another man landed next to him. Feroz rolled to the right as the man snatched the leads from his hand. He opened the spring clamp of the arc welder ground, and fixed it to the support arm. With his other hand, the man pulled a long welding rod from the top of his drenched boot.

Feroz felt the tanker rise and knew the seas would once more swarm in like an assassin. He reached over and clamped his powerful arms around the man's legs. An instant later, the horrid white wall of water sprang at them.

Feroz felt the submarine lurch to port, as his lungs fought to keep the salty ocean from killing him. A flash of light stabbed in the water. As if it had been stung, the water roared away. Feroz opened his eyes and saw the flashes of light became one bright glow. Sparks hissed through the air and sizzled as they hit the wet deck.

Feroz felt the steel support arm stiffen. Another flash of light seared into his eyes, as another wave washed down upon the two men.

"Secured, Captain," the man shouted over the frothing water.

Feroz released his grip and struggled to his knees. The unknown welder timed the next rise of water. When the surge ended, he crawled, one hand following the other along the support beam until he reached the end attached to the side of the shell.

Feroz also timed the next watery assault. The wave came and the tanker's bow climbed. The water retreated as his powerful legs pushed toward SIMCER's sail and shelter.

Mystic, Connecticut

Ice and snow, driven by gusts of gale-like air,

tapped at the frosted windows as if jealous of the warmth inside.

Here, it was quiet. The air smelled of the hot cinnamon rolls Jennifer had baked earlier. Yet, though the air was warm, a heavy chill hung in the house. Something unseen and dreaded had come home with Grant McKinnon.

Misty could tell all was not well. The usually playful child seemed content to huddle with her crayons and coloring book.

Jennifer had done wonders with the fresh salmon. Broiled to perfection with a lemon pepper glaze, served over rice with steamed squash. She had indeed done her best though McKinnon had hardly tasted any of it.

He carried the dishes to the kitchen. Jennifer followed. "Grant," she said softly as she took his hand in hers. 'I know this is new to both of us." She wrapped an arm around his neck. "If this is going to work, you have to trust me. Now tell me, what's wrong?"

McKinnon looked down into those warm and wonderful eyes. Her hand, soft and tender in his own rough palm, seemed as if it could soothe any trouble. Guilt once more slithered up his spine.

He had let one woman down. One child had died alone and cold. They'd told him Danny had died instantly, but McKinnon had always wondered. Now fate wanted another chance at his soul. He could only stare back into those deep understanding eyes that were like windows to the past. "I love you," he whispered his lips barely moving.

"Is that the problem?" Jennifer asked softly as she stroked his face.

McKinnon felt himself surrender. A door opened in his mind, freeing something long trapped. He looked again and saw only Jennifer and felt her hand on his cheek.

From somewhere in his brain, a thought flashed. *This time, you can save them.* "No problem at all, Jen," he smiled as he pressed his lips into hers.

Chapter Nineteen

THE FIRST TIME

"In a minute there is time
for decisions and revisions
which a minute will reverse."
~T.S. Eliot

Lapadnaya Lista
Russian Submarine Base
January 13th

He had told her not to. She knew he would be upset, still, there she stood as she had so often in her life.

A crumbled wall of rotted blocks that had once been used to obscure the pier now provided Evelina Danyankov concealment. She hoped her husband would not see her.

From here, she had watched her father sail off into the Arctic and beyond.

When she was small and had not

understood, it was better. Then, it was almost fun. The handsome proud sailors lined up like tin soldiers on the submarine's deck. Some would wave and blow kisses to her.

Now that she was grown and did understand, it was a far different feeling.

A shrill blast from one of two squat tugboats sliced through the silence. Evelina watched as the dirty smoky vessels nudged alongside her husbands' sleek, deadly looking submarine.

Tears froze on her eyelashes as she watched men on the tugs feed the heavy lines to sailors on the submarine's deck. "No turning back now," She breathed into the cold still air.

More shrill whistles and the tugboats chugged forward. Plumes of gray-black smoke erupted from the stubby funnels as the lines grew taut. Slowly, VEPR moved away from the old neglected pier.

Evelina wiped her gloved hand across her eyes. She could hear the crunch as ice cracked and fell from the rounded black hull.

Once it was in the channel, she watched the lines splash into the ice-choked water, and the tugboats hurriedly waddle away as if afraid of what they had set free.

A greenish-white froth boiled from under the AKULA's stern as the screw tasted water. The surge subsided and the submarine slid toward open water. A ghostly mist gathered around the submarine, as it increased speed. A slight ripple of white formed near the rounded bow.

High above, seabirds swung screaming into formation as if to guide her husband away.

She watched as VEPR rounded the entrance to the main harbor. As the hull grew smaller, she stared at the now empty pier. She looked up just in time to see VEPR disappear beyond the low snow-covered hills.

"Please come home," she whispered.

Aboard the Iranian Oil Tanker
Behzad Nabavi
The Atlantic

Under normal circumstances, the promotion would have been a blessing from Allah himself.

His name and picture would appear on the front page of his hometown newspaper. There would be parties, a grand dinner with plates of *Beryani*, and trays of *Tah Cheen*.

He thought of his mother. She would not really understand what an Engineer did, but she would be proud.

However, these circumstances were anything but normal. His promotion occurred in the chilled cavern of steel. There was no ceremony, no congratulations.

Commander Feroz had called him to the top level of the shell and spoke only four words. "You are now Engineer."

The furious sea had calmed to stillness in the early hours.

Feroz's newly appointed Engineer hurried

through each of SIMCER's compartments checking for damages. Other than a few shattered pieces of kitchenware, the submarine seemed unharmed.

Frigid water of the Mid-Atlantic winter now surrounded the tanker's lumbering hull. In the steel shell, temperatures plummeted as the metal surrendered its heat. At first, the chill had been a pleasant relief from the sweltering broiler of before.

By afternoon, the simple act of breathing caused a foggy mist. That mist and the glow of the weak fluorescent bulbs gave the atmosphere the appearance of a nightmare.

The men did what they could to find comfort. Around their emaciated shoulders they draped thin damp wool blankets that reeked of rot and mildew. Men, who only days before had cursed the heat, now shivered in the cold.

Pier 12
Naval Submarine Base
Groton, Connecticut
January 14th

The winter sky cleared a bit along the Thames River. Patches of blue managed to sneak through the gray overcast. A few rays of the long gone sun took advantage of the gap in the winter clouds to shine over the ice and snow.

For the first time since the middle of

December, the temperature crept just above freezing. Along every eave water dripped from icicles and splashed to the dirty snow below.

Towards the upper end of the Submarine Base, USS MIAMI SSN 755 rode gently at her berth. The submarine's long proud black profile stood in marked contrast to the snow and ice that surrounded her. The long gentle curve of her bow and purposeful square sail gave the vessel a regal look, as she stood ready to free herself from land.

The Deck Gang sent down the last topside gear. Lifelines, stanchions, hatch-covers, vent covers, all cleared and neatly stowed below.

Torpedomen checked the twelve vertical launch missile tube hatches. Auxiliary Division removed the sanitary connection, took in the potable water line, and installed a new ceramic diffuser for the CO_2 overboard.

At the head of the pier, just outside the 15-foot chain link fence, the MIAMI's Captain said his goodbyes.

"How do I do this?" Jennifer asked as tears streaked down her cheeks.

Grant McKinnon had been asking himself the same question all morning. "It's not like I'm going forever," he offered. "Two weeks tops."

Misty lifted her arms and he snatched her up tightly. *Don't know if I can let go!*

"You will be back tonight?" She begged hopefully.

"No, Little One," he answered seriously. "But

I will come back as soon as I can."

"Will you see any whales?"

McKinnon had to smile. "I guess we could."

Misty turned her head to her mother. Her face suddenly still. "You're going after the bad guys, aren't you!"

McKinnon felt his heart drop. His smile faded. *How could she know?* The guilt nipped at him. "What bad guys?"

Now a tear dropped from the corner of the child's eye. "I don't know," she whimpered. "My tummy tells me."

From the place in the soul where matters of the heart tell not only the truth, they shout it, a voice whispered, *She loves you.*

Grant McKinnon swallowed hard. He searched his memory for the right words. He then understood something he had known all along, but forgotten. There are no right words. "Well, you tell that tummy of yours not to worry." He kissed her cheek and set her down on the cold concrete of the pier. "Do me a favor," he said as he learned close to her ear. "If Mommy gets sad, will you do something to make her smile?"

"I sure will," Misty sniffled. "I do lots of stuff to make her smile."

McKinnon reached for Jennifer's hand. "You don't worry either, Jen."

"Can't promise that," she replied as she wiped the tears from her face.

McKinnon's head turned as Admiral

Tarrent's car crunched along the narrow ice-covered road. With a muffled squeak of the brakes, the car stopped short of the pier head.

Tarrent smiled warmly as he stepped from the car. He squared his white peaked combination cap on his head. "Hello Jennifer."

"Hello, Burke," she replied with as much a smile as she could.

"Commander, if I can have a word."

Reluctantly, McKinnon released Jennifer's hand and stepped to Tarrent's car.

"Just received a report on that Iranian sailor they found on the bottom." Tarrent's face suddenly carried the look of worry that over the years had carved deep lines around his mouth.

"Yes, sir?"

"That was no sailor," Tarrent sighed.

"Tell me more, Admiral."

"Forensics found a tattoo on the inside of his lower lip. It translated as freedom."

"He was a plant?"

"We think so," Tarrent nodded. "If they went to that much trouble, this thing's bigger than we thought."

McKinnon remained silent.

Tarrent's eyes narrowed. "Are you sure there's nothing else I need to know?"

"Trust me, no." McKinnon answered.

"Don't have much of a choice, eh?" Tarrent looked toward the river. "Tugs are coming."

McKinnon came to attention and saluted. "Request permission to get underway."

Admiral Tarrent returned the salute. "Permission granted."

McKinnon returned to Jennifer and Misty. "I have to go now," he said as he kissed each tenderly. "You be good and remember what I asked," he said as he bent to stroke Misty's chin. Before she could speak, he left them and hurried through the gate onto the pier.

Tarrent walked over to where Jennifer stood trembling. "First time's always the worst."

"You mean it gets easier?"

"No," he growled. "I hope it never does."

Misty reached for the Admiral's hand. "He's going to be okay, isn't he?"

Tarrent looked down at her big, sad eyes. "Do you like spaghetti?" He asked.

"Who doesn't?"

"How about lunch? My treat."

Jennifer's eyes turned back to the river. The tugs were tied alongside MIAMI's sleek black hull. "I should wait..."

"No, you shouldn't," Tarrent said firmly, taking her arm. "Come on. I know a great little pasta place near here. Fills up fast at lunch."

"I don't like peppers," Misty warned, skipping along beside him, holding his hand.

"Me neither," Admiral Tarrent smiled as he helped them into the car. After he shut the doors, he looked toward MIAMI as the tugs eased her away from the pier. "He'll be just fine," he growled to himself.

Chapter Twenty

THE UNKNOWN

*"All our knowledge
merely helps us to die
a more painful death
than animals that know nothing."*
~Maurice Maeterlinck

The Pentagon
Washington, DC

Defense Secretary Martin Samuels drummed his fingers nervously on the top of his desk. "We're taking a beating."

"How so?" Chairman of the Joint Chiefs of Staff Malroy asked.

"Come on, Jim," Samuels sighed. "You read the papers. The Dems are screaming bloody murder on defense spending."

"That's nothing new." Malroy shrugged.

"We can't give 'em a good reason why we

need the money," Samuels slapped his palm on the desktop. "After that U-boat affair, everyone thinks it's over. All the world's problems solved, just like that!" He snapped his fingers. "Everyone loves everyone."

"So tell 'em," Malroy retorted.

Samuels smiled thinly. "We just go ahead and tell Mr. John Q Public why we need two submarines a year. Why we keep the carriers at sea. Why we need three more infantry divisions. Then we get jumped for our lousy foreign relations."

Malroy crossed his legs. "Mr. Secretary, with all due respect, I don't care."

"We could lose this election," Samuels taunted.

"Yes sir, you could."

"Then what?" Samuels asked.

"You tell me, Mr. Secretary," Malroy countered.

Samuels rubbed his forehead. "You know what they want to do with the Military. We'll be lucky to get a submarine once a decade."

"There *are* smart people in both parties," Malroy offered. "I'll even bet some on the other side of the aisle are just as patriotic as you, Mr. Secretary. Besides, John Q ain't stupid."

Samuels took a moment to fidget with his pen. "I've heard rumors about an Iranian submarine."

"We don't work off of rumors, Mr. Secretary," Malroy responded.

"Well, they should have come to me through you," Samuels grumbled.

"Like I said, we don't work off of rumors."

Secretary Samuels eyes focused on the Chairman of the Joint Chiefs of Staff. "CIA thinks the whole thing's a sham."

"Now why would they think that?"

"Jim!" Samuels all but yelled. "This is no time to play dodge ball."

Admiral Malroy hoisted his six-foot, seven-inch frame out of the chair. In two steps, he towered over the Secretary of Defense. "You are correct," he growled. "This is the time to take off your political party hat and be an American."

Samuels leaned back as the huge Texan loomed over him. When the anger drained from his eyes it was replaced with fear. "What's going on, Jim?"

"If there's anything to these rumors, I'll let you know," Malroy backed off, allowing the shaken politician some room. "Is that all, sir?" He asked politely.

Secretary of Defense Samuels pulled the handkerchief from his breast pocket and dabbed at the sweat on his hairline. "It is, Chairman."

Malroy's face relaxed. "I'll keep you informed, Mr. Secretary." He left the office, letting the door click shut behind him.

Ellis Island, New York Harbor

At the southeastern edge of the tiny dot of land, thirty-feet down upon the gentle slope of sand, mud and rock, the weapon waited.

The propulsion section had mostly rotted and rusted away. Only the drive shaft, drive gears and twin bronze screws remained.

The stainless steel warhead, though tarnished, was unaffected by time or the salt water that had flowed around it for more than forty years.

The perfect sphere of plutonium nestled deep in its protective case slowly decayed. This decay produced heat, which in turn kept small sets of batteries charged. A simple sensor circuit monitored minute changes in the amperage draw and signaled the release of heat from the warhead pit into a chemical that absorbed the few electrons that escaped. Like a capacitor, the chemical reached a saturation point, then released the electrons into the batteries.

The batteries served three functions. First, it fed eleven milliamps to a wire coil that formed small loops around the weapon case.

Wired in series and set along the interior, small mercury switches were joined to the wires at points where any abrupt movement of more than 30 degrees in yaw or pitch would shut and send a signal to the firing circuit. These loops of wire also kept a small charge on the shell of the weapon itself. Should someone attempt to cut into it, the field of passing electrons would be interrupted and a magnetic switch held open by the tiny voltage would shut, sending the signal and needed voltage to the detonator.

The batteries also operated a simple timer. At random intervals every thirty days, it switched on a set of miniature electric motors. Connected to these motors small wheels, surrounded by soft synthetic rubber, spun at 600 rpm. These wheels were set into machined recesses in a tube of stainless steel. The tube followed a path around the shell in curves and dips until it reached the point it started. Within the tube, three titanium ball bearings squeezed into the wheels and shot through the tube. As they snaked through the tube, they caused the warhead to vibrate. This vibration cleared the warheads exterior of silt or mud.

Atop the warhead, the batteries fed power to three inlaid ceramic hydrophones. Each was set to receive a different frequency of sound energy, connected to a set of primitive reed switches. When proper frequencies vibrated across the ceramic sound heads, the reed switches closed. Should all three close in the programmed order, voltage would surge to the firing circuit, detonating the warhead.

It lay there in the murky silt, as it had for decades, waiting and listening.

Aboard the Russian AKULA Class
K-157 VEPR

Rocks hewn by long gone glaciers towered over
VEPR as she made her last turn toward the
open sea. The water that swirled around her
bow and danced in a froth at her rounded
sides, slowly turned from the gray-green of the
polluted harbor to a dark, rich blue.

Fishermen whose small worn crafts bobbed
and heaved at the mercy of VEPR's roiling
wake, cursed as the sleek submarine sped
past.

With the outline of the Kola Peninsula still
visible and only 150 meters beneath her keel,
Commander Danyankov ordered the submarine
under the sea. VEPR's 12,770 tons of gracefully
curved steel slithered into the Arctic Ocean.

Aboard the Iranian Oil Tanker
Behzad Nabavi
650 Nautical Miles From
New York City

Conditions in the shell took a toll not only on the
men. Streaks of rust now fanned down the
KILO's squat tower. Along the stubby hull rust
also collected in random spots like scabs from
some plague. The bridge windows frosted over
in the rancid cold air. Like dead eyes, they
looked down on the miserable men.

Asha Feroz became ghost-like in the narrow

confines of the shell. Alone he took his ration of cold rice and processed chicken. He issued few orders. He left the ordinary work to the officers. with the strict understanding that if he had to be involved, it meant they had failed. Each officer knew from Feroz's reputation that men rarely survived failure.

In the small chamber near the hatch, SIMCER's commander spent his days. He called to the tanker's bridge every four hours for a position report. He recorded the tanker's progress on the now warped and blotched chart spread on the sheet metal table. He slept only in brief naps.

Today, men whose own eyes were sunken deep within their skulls, watched as Feroz eased himself down the ladder.

"Engineer," he called.

Newly-appointed to his post, the young officer stood to attention. "Sir?" He croaked.

Feroz's scarred vocal cords, rasped in a deep sickly resonance. "Tomorrow is the day. Have the ship and men ready." He offered a grimace of a smile. "Then we will be out of this hellhole."

"Sir?" The new Engineer spoke like a condemned man with nothing to lose.

"What is it?" Feroz snarled.

"The plan, sir. What is it?"

Feroz stared down at the slimy steel diamond deck. "Our plan is to detach from this coffin. We'll stay deep a few days, warm up, get some hot food, then proceed with our mission."

The Engineer swallowed hard. "What is our mission, sir?"

Feroz's head swung slowly up. He aimed the black pits that were his eyes at the young officer.

The new Engineer's eyelids fluttered as he watched the scar on Feroz's face. The line traced by the two-decade-old wound seemed to glow and pulse in the putrid mist.

"Our mission is to do our duty." Feroz eyes now narrowed into slits. Still, the darkness of the black pupils reached out. "Is there another question?"

"No, Captain," the young officer shivered. "The ship and men will be ready."

USS MIAMI SSN 755

She passed silently and with little notice from the mouth of the Thames River, and into Block Island Sound.

High above, wisps of gray finally won as they crowded out the patches of blue.

Once clear of the Block Island lighthouse, Commander Grant McKinnon brought MIAMI's engines to a full bell. The bow pushed through the water so precisely, the unbroken surface tension rolled up and over the perfectly shaped sonar dome.

A lonely Atlantic white-sided dolphin joined in formation as MIAMI made for her dive point. The 600 pound mammal leapt in graceful arcs as it rode the pressure wave formed by the submarine's passage.

Now clear of land and with no close contacts to worry with, McKinnon sat alone at the small desk in his stateroom. He checked his watch. *Time for Misty's bath.* Just to have that to think about made him smile. A gentle rap at the door brought him back to where he really was.

"Enter," he said softly.

Executive Officer Lieutenant Commander Bradley Gellor stepped in.

"How's the leg?" McKinnon asked.

"This weather makes it a bit stiff, but nothing I can't handle," Gellor replied with a grin. "So, Skipper, what's the tasking?"

McKinnon exhaled slowly. "It's a strange one, this time."

"How so?"His XO chuckled. "What could be stranger than a German U-boat come back to life?"

"Trust me," McKinnon answered as his face grew serious. "This is big league stuff."

"You're worried," Gellor murmured. "I can tell."

"Brad, we're going hunting."

Gellor's head cocked to the side. "For what?"

McKinnon shook his head, "I don't know."

"You're losing me, Skipper," Gellor said, a crease forming between his eyebrows.

"Okay, here it is," McKinnon leaned back in his chair. "There's a nuclear weapon somewhere in New York Harbor..."

"Say again?" Gellor interrupted.

"Let me finish!" McKinnon soothed him. "We think the Iranians are going attempt to detonate it."

The XO's eyes went wide. "How could they do that? They can't even get to sea. Didn't they just sink one of their..." Then his face twisted as he fit the pieces together.

McKinnon nodded. "It didn't sink."

Gellor's head bobbed as his brain processed what his ears had just told him. "A nuke going off in the harbor would wipe out most of the city," Gellor hissed. "New Jersey—gone." His eyes blinked. "Groton."

"I know, Brad," McKinnon said softly.

Gellor's voice now trembled. "We're sending out only the one boat?"

"This is where it gets tricky, XO," McKinnon whispered. "The President and SECDEF don't know about this."

"They don't?" Gellor's whole body went on alert.

McKinnon lifted his palms, "Calm down, Brad."

"Calm down?" Gellor protested, rubbing his jaw. "We're talking about Groton, Skipper. You don't have family there any—" Too late, Gellor caught himself . "Sorry, sir." He lowered his head. "I... I'm such a jerk sometimes."

"I understand," McKinnon replied, making an effort at a smile. "It's all about politics,

Brad, and more than you or I need to know."

"Why only us?" Gellor sighed.

"It's not just us," McKinnon murmured.

The Executive Officer's head cocked to the side. "Didn't see anyone else on the boards."

"No, you didn't," McKinnon replied.

"A boat out of Norfolk?"

McKinnon shook his head. "No."

"Who else is there?"

McKinnon rubbed his face, then looked up at his XO, "Danyankov."

Chapter Twenty-One

HUNTERS AND THE HUNTED

"Who can hope to be safe?
Who sufficiently cautious?
Guard himself as he may,
every moment's an ambush."
~Horace

Tehran, Iran
January 15th

The door opened into a small room, devoid of color or life, where the old cleric sat alone in the sickly yellow glow from a window pane set high in the ocher painted block walls.

Seated with his back to the door, his dark robes flowing from his shoulders over the beige cushions to the floor, the old cleric had been waiting for him. Beside him on a low table of worn pine were a leather bound copy of the Koran and a cell phone.

"What is your news?" Ayatollah Majeed Ali Sohrab asked in his familiar, nasal drone.

President Mehran let the heavy door click shut behind him. "It will happen in five days." He stood staring at the old cleric's back, waiting for orders.

Sohrab did not move. "Five days."

"Yes," The moment Mehran had stepped into this room he had sensed a dread that set his heart thudding, making his mouth dry.

"You will remain here until it is done," the old man ordered.

"But my duties..." Mehran protested, feeling for the door handle.

The old man remained still. "Are here. You will make your peace with Allah."

"But the people need me!" The President tried again.

"You will serve the people, here." Ayatollah Sohrab crooned.

Sweat broke out on Mehran's forehead. "And... should it fail?" He whispered.

"Then, also, you will serve the people."

Russian Akula Class
K-157 VEPR

Invisible in the black water that rushed along her sleek deadly form, the Russian attack submarine surged northwest.

In the command center, Captain First Rank Valerik Danyankov studied the newly updated digital chart. The numbers told an ugly truth. VEPR would need every knot the VM-5 reactor could produce if there was any hope of intercepting the tanker.

He pushed the cursor of the digital map to the west. The image tracked along until it reached an area 1000 nautical miles from the coast of the United States. *Where?* Danyankov scanned the broad expanse.

The Varshavyanka had a range of 400 miles at 5 knots. Danyankov pressed another menu button on the digital panel. The screen blanked for a second, then the word CURRENTS appeared. VEPR's Commander pushed the select button and a list of the world's ocean currents popped up. He moved his finger over the mouse wheel until the curser highlighted GULF STREAM. Again, his index finger touched the enter button.

The information flashed across the screen. Now the numbers gave him a tiny touch of hope. With the Gulf Stream's three-knot current, that would cut him down to 2 knots.

"Captain," a voice in the dimness called.

"What is it?" Danyankov growled.

"Sir, before we submerged, we received this intelligence report."

"Go on."

"A Norwegian diesel submarine is operating in this area."

Danyankov turned and snatched the report from the unseen operator's outstretched hand.

He held it next to the display panel. *We have been moving too fast to hear a very quiet diesel boat. If he hears us, word will be out!*

Danyankov went over the options in his mind. *Slow down and lose time. Continue at 26 knots and if this Norwegian is any good, he'll snap us up.* Then another thought flashed through. *We could run him over. At this speed, a collision would sink one—possibly both of us.*

Danyankov searched the part of his brain where his bag of tricks was cached. "Sonar," he called. "What contacts do you hold?"

"Sir, we hold no contacts of interest," came the reply.

"I asked what contacts?" Danyankov roared.

"Uh, sir, we hold numerous fishing vessels bearing 282."

"Identify!" Danyankov barked.

"Sir, transients classified as fishing gear and engine noises. Sounds like deep sea trawlers."

"Come to new course 280," VEPR's Captain ordered.

Gracefully, the Russian submarine swung to her new course.

"Captain!" The Navigator warned, "You have five minutes on this heading before we enter Norwegian territorial waters."

Royal Norwegian Naval Submarine
S305 UREDD
6 Miles Southeast

Captain Eyjolf thoughtfully stirred the lump of sugar into his steaming cup of tea.

The day had gone well. The crew had shaken off the rust of too much time in port. The fire and emergency drills were not too bad. His officers did a fair job during the attack simulations. Tomorrow, the ship would run rabbit for some ASW helicopters, then head back in.

Eyjolf made his night order entry in the log, then slouched in the seat of his small cabin. He'd picked up the tea mug just as the buzzer to the Control Room phone sounded.

"Yes?" he said into the handset. He listened without comment, then replaced the handset in its holder.

Thirty seconds later, tea forgotten, Eyjolf stood in the Control Room. "Are you sure?" He demanded.

"Yes sir," the Watch Officer nodded. "82 and 64 Hertz tonal bearing 020."

Eyjolf frowned. "Bearing rate?"

"It calculates to 25 knots, sir."

"Where is it now?" UREDD's Captain asked.

"Faded. Last bearing 013. It merged, then I lost it in the noise from that fishing fleet."

"Can't be what you thought!" Eyjolf grimaced. "No Russian submarine, especially that one, would run so carelessly into a group of trawlers."

"But the tonal signal matched," the Watch Officer objected.

"Things are not always as they seem," Eyjolf sneered. "Think about it, Lars. If it were the VEPR, he would now be in our waters."

The Watch Officer shook his head. "Yes sir, but..."

Eyjolf cut him off, "Rumors may have it the VEPR's Captain is crazy. Not crazy enough, I think, to violate our space."

"I was sure, sir," the Watch Officer said reluctantly.

"You did the right thing," Eyjolf nodded. "Better safe than sorry, eh?" He patted the young officer on the shoulder. "I'm off to bed."

Aboard the Iranian Oil Tanker
Behzad Nabavi
430 Nautical Miles From
New York City

You understand if you are slow, you will stay here?" Feroz rasped at the five men, waiting for each to nod. "Man your stations then," SIMCER"S Commander rasped.

The men shuffled away as quickly as their weak legs would carry them. Four scurried to the ends of the support arms connecting their submarine to the tanker. The fifth carefully climbed the slippery steel ladder to the small chamber at the top of the shell.

"Engineer," Feroz growled into the bridge microphone. "Make ready to submerge."

Office of Naval Intelligence
Washington, DC

Commander Sills stared at the hands of the large clock jerking the minutes away.

Another five and the night shift would take over. The day had been pretty much routine, which in military terms translated to boredom of the tenth magnitude.

To pass the last few moments of her watch, Sills scanned the wire service teletype machines. "Same old same old," she yawned as her eyes ran over the headlines from around the planet.

Again she looked at the clock. "Game starts at seven," she muttered.

"Kid have a game tonight?" Lieutenant TO asked.

"First of the playoffs," Sills answered.

TO smiled as he logged off his computer. "How old is she now?"

"My baby Brianna is fourteen, but thinks she's thirty," Sills snorted.

"Mine turns five next we..." The secure phone buzzed.

Sills rounded her desk to the shelf with one of five multi-colored telephones. She picked up the receiver for the phone dedicated to the United States Coast Guard. "Commander Sills," she answered.

As she listened, she took a pen from the pocket of her jacket and jotted notes on the pad

234 D. Clayton Meadows

attached to the shelf. "I have the information and will pass it along." When the line went dead, she replaced the receiver.

"Anything interesting?" Lieutenant TO asked as he stretched.

"An Iranian tanker... ah, let me see if I can say this correctly... *Behzad Nabavi* reported trouble with their rudder and is stopped to make repairs."

"Those boys just can't catch a break," TO rubbed his face. "First, they lose a sub, and now this."

"Here's their latest fix," Sills said as she handed TO her notes.

"I've already shut down." He complained.

"Then leave a note for the night crew."

"Will do," TO placed the note on the computer keyboard and got to his feet.

USS MIAMI SSN 755
200 Nautical Miles Northeast of New York Harbor

Although he knew he desperately needed it, sleep eluded Grant McKinnon as he sprawled in his bunk. Tactics, sound velocity profiles and weapon settings crowded his skull, warding off the weariness that ached at his eyes.

Who's out there? He asked the darkness of his stateroom. When no answer came, his thoughts turned to Jennifer. He hoped they would chase away the complex calculations, and allow him to drift off into blessed sleep.

In his mind's eye, he saw her laugh, saw her brush the hair from her face. Saw her focus her soft eyes on him. At last, McKinnon felt his body relax.

Then he saw Misty, and the cute way she wrinkled her nose when vegetables were put on her plate. He could almost hear her "Eeeuw!"

McKinnon's eyes closed. He saw Jennifer and Misty walking toward him, both reaching out for him, their smiles radiating their own warm light.

McKinnon snuggled into his blanket. He could feel sleep wash over him. His body was sinking deep into a welcoming soft mattress.

Then he saw the cloud. Black and malignant, it rose behind Jennifer and Misty. It swirled, and began to chase them.

McKinnon yelled a warning, but no sound came from his mouth. He could hear the cloud as it buzzed with a menacing static. Radiation.

He tried to run to them, but his feet would not obey. He tried to pull at his legs but they were too heavy to move.

The cloud grew higher and thicker. The static buzz filled his ears. The cloud reared up and fell upon them and their mouths opened and thick streams of blood flowed out.

Paralyzed, McKinnon could only watch as Misty's face seemed to melt, the radiation tearing the cells of her very being to shreds.

Jennifer wilted and withered. Her beautiful eyes glazed over with a dark ugly film. Then she crumpled to the ground and evaporated in a sudden explosion of ashes.

McKinnon woke up gasping. He shook his head to get rid of the terrible images. He shivered as cool air from the ventilation system washed over his sweat-drenched face.

He collapsed back in his bunk, and stared into the dark again. *Who's out there?*

Chapter Twenty-Two

BUMPS IN THE NIGHT

*"He has not learned the lesson of life
who does not every day
surmount a fear."*
~Ralph Waldo Emerson

Russian Attack Submarine
K-157 VEPR

As the noise of the fishing fleet faded, VEPR moved southwest into the cold expanse of the Norwegian Sea. She cleared the shallows near Namsos, where the ocean floor dropped to 500 meters.

In the dim light of the command center, figures moved about like silent phantoms. It was still and peaceful with only a slight vibration as the smooth laminar hull cleaved through the sea.

"Sonar, be alert for surface contacts," Danyankov ordered. "We will use large merchants for cover."

In the thin light, the Engineering Officer entered the command center. "Captain, the number one hydraulic oil cooler filter is a bit hot. I would like to slow and change it out."

"We cannot slow down," Danyankov responded. "Bypass the filter if you have to, but we will not decrease speed."

"That could be dangerous," the Engineer replied.

"Danger is for us to slow down," Danyankov replied coldly.

Iranian Submarine
SIMCER

The shudders and groans of the tanker's hull eased as she lost headway.

Commander Feroz craned his short neck over the side of the sail. He watched as the surge and gurgle of the water that passed under the tanker subsided.

"Release," he shouted to the four men positioned at the connect points of the support arms. Each hammered furiously at the thick steel pins. Soon, he heard a loud splash and then another as one by one the connecting pins fell into the water.

Now supported by her own buoyancy, the SIMCER bobbed in the tiny steel harbor.

Footsteps rang on the submarine's flat deck as the five men raced toward the after casing hatch. The tiny submarine rolled slightly and caused one of the men to fall hard on the rough diamond deck. For the two behind him, there was no time to stop and they too tumbled hard onto the unyielding steel.

Feroz heard their shrieks of pain and turned. "Get up," his rasped. "We dive in two minutes, with or without you."

The first of the men stopped and turned, he moved carefully back the way he had come and helped the men to their feet. Bloodied and limping, they reached the hatch. Man after wounded man, they climbed from one steel coffin into another.

In the cold swirls of mist, Feroz took a last look at the steel cavern that had been their lair for far too long. "Submerge!" He ordered as he slid down into the bridge hatch.

The bridge cover and hatch clanged shut just as the ballast tank vents opened. Plumes of tormented water rose in eruptions of foam as water replaced the air in the KILO's ballast tanks.

SIMCER settled gently, first the hull dipped below, then the squat sail sank. Remnants of trapped air freed themselves in car-sized bubbles, as the pressure of the sea forced them from the flood grates and limber holes.

The small Russian-built submarine drifted slowly beneath the tanker. At 15 meters, the five-bladed screws began to turn and she pushed forward away from the hulk overhead.

USS MIAMI SSN 755

In the Control Center, the watch standers went about their duties as directed by the Captain's night orders. In Sonar, highly trained technicians listened to the seething sea.

The messenger of the watch had just brought up coffee when MIAMI's electronic ear caught something.

"Conn, Sonar," the Sonar Supervisor reported. "Sonar gained new contact, on passive narrow band PPB-2 designate contact Sierra 17. Sierra 17 classified as heavy merchant by nature of sound." There was a pause.

"Sonar, Conn," the Officer of the Deck called out. "Can you give me a turn rate?"

"Conn, Sonar, this is a distant contact. We might be having some masking problems. Turn count was initially 78 RPM on two five-bladed screws."

Information was automatically sent to the BSY-1 Fire Control screen. The Officer of the Deck checked the new icon that designated Sierra 17. "Way out there, Sonar," the Officer of the Deck commented.

"Conn, Sonar, aye. Based on bottom bounce, this contact..."

"What is it, Sonar?" the Officer of the Deck

asked into the open microphone.

"Conn, Sonar estimate this contact to be greater than 100 miles. We are detecting heavy transients from Sierra 17." Again, there was a pause. "Turn rate is down to 0."

"Zero?" the Officer of the Deck repeated.

"Yes sir. Believe the contact has stopped."

"Can you classify the transients?"

"Conn, Sonar, aye. We hold numerous metallic noises and air."

The Office of the Deck looked puzzled. "You think the merchant is in trouble?"

"Conn, Sonar, wait," the Sonar Supervisor replied. "Conn, Sierra 17 has started again. She is making 22 turns. Transients have faded."

"Okay, Sonar," the Officer of the Deck sighed. "Watch Sierra 17."

K-157 VEPR

Captain First Rank Valerik Danyankov sat alone in his cabin. In his hand, he held the picture Evelina had given him at Christmas.

The old photo was somehow comforting, a link, and a bond with something he had never really understood. *Did you ever dream your mission would effect me and your grandson?' Would you have still carried it out?* Danyankov's mind answered his own question. *I would have.*

Tenderly, he set the picture in the back corner of the desk. *Tell me, Poppa, which route would you take?*

Iceland formed a natural obstacle for the Russian submarine. There were two ways to go in order to gain access to the coast of North America. Around the northern tip of Iceland and down through the Denmark Strait would be his first choice. There, the ocean divided into a vast array of temperature layers. The best route for a silent approach. The two problems with this route would be the close proximity to St. George's Bank and the Canadian Maritimes. Should he be detected, NATO would definitely take notice. Then there were the fishing fleets that flocked to the area. Encountering a net or worse, sinking one of the trawlers would end the mission.

Far more dangerous, but quicker, was the route south around Iceland. Here the acoustic profile of the deep water was perfect for hunting. The bad news was it was just as good for being hunted. The Americans operated P-3s off Iceland. Although he would stay deep and fast, there was always the chance some hotshot pilot could get lucky.

Which way, Poppa? He stared at the photograph. Something caught his eye. He studied the picture up close. His father had been cradling him in his right arm. In his left hand, he held a book. A children's book.

Memories flooded back in waves. He remembered it was the first book his mother had given him. She had taught him to read with it. Even now, he could recall the entire simple text. In his mind, he could see the delicate watercolor paintings that helped tell the story of a family of polar bears who wanted a new home away from the cold of the north. "*The Bears Go South,*" he whispered the title.

He raised the picture closer. His father's hand covered all the words of the title but two, Go South.

For most of his adult life, the word "family" had little meaning for Valerik Danyankov. Now he realized it meant everything.

A chill snaked up his spine. *I hope I can save mine.*

Chapter Twenty-Three

WORST CASE SCENARIOS

*"Who so diggeth a pit shall fall therein:
and he that rolleth a stone,
it will return upon him."*
~Proverbs 26:27

Iranian KILO Class Submarine
SIMCER
January 16th

She moved slowly in the darkness of the deep Atlantic, her every move cautious and planned.

Only at night did she near the surface to gulp in the cold moist air and recharge her batteries. Like a vampire, she returned to the dark when the light came.

Inside the cramped submarine, the crew regained their strength. Lungs choked with the foul noxious air of the shell, now welcomed the fresh air that circulated freely. Stomachs that

ached from lack of nutrition, were now filled
with good hot food.

At the small table of his closet-sized cabin,
Commander Asha Feroz plotted his approach.
He would come in from the south, where New
York Harbor was deepest. If undetected, he
would proceed until the water depth forced him
to stop. He circled a location on the chart
where he would bottom SIMCER and carry out
his mission.

Just for curiosity's sake, he scanned the
faded chart for any bottom feature that might
protect SIMCER from the blast. He thanked
Allah that he found none.

He reached up and felt the scar on his face.
He let his fingers trace along the gash that had
taken 300 stitches to close. *Soon, all the pain
will be gone.*

K-157 VEPR

So far, VEPR remained unseen and unheard as
she rushed southwest.

The hull-mounted sonar array had detected
the presence of a distant Canadian frigate last
night. Captain First Rank Danyankov had
maneuvered between layers just in case the
passive system on the small warship got a sniff.

VEPR neared the North American shelf in
the early hours.

Surface traffic picked up as she entered the
shipping lanes off Halifax, and Danyankov

hoped the presence of the plodding merchants meant he was still a secret. *Where is McKinnon,? Did he believe me? Would I?*

For an instant, Danyankov toyed with the idea of coming to periscope depth. It would take only seconds to receive any updates on the tanker's location.

He also knew that in those few seconds his cover could be blown. A mast exposed too long, a loss of depth control sticking the conning tower out of the water. *Risk management.*

For the first time, Danyankov thought about the Varshavyanka, what McKinnon called a KILO. *Who was in command?*

Years ago, he had given the Persians a lecture in combat use of isothermal layers. Afterwards, he met with them to review their performance in tactical exercises.

He remembered only a handful of officers. Their names long forgotten. One had done spectacularly poorly on the test. But the other had been a competent enough submariner, even completed the course with high marks. Still, Danyankov could not see that man commanding a mission like this. No heart for battle, as he recalled.

Then the image of a short man came into focus. The one who'd been shunned by his fellow officers. The one with that grotesque injury. Suddenly his name popped up in Danyankov's memory. "Feroz!" He said it aloud. *Scar Face.*

Then he remembered how well Feroz had handled the small and nimble Varshavyanka submarine.

USS MIAMI SSN 755

Just after dawn, Commander Grant McKinnon brought MIAMI to periscope depth. The sea had picked up some. White-capped waves of three or more feet washed over the thin optic window of the number two periscope. The Diving Officer nudged the 6,900-ton submarine a few feet closer to the surface. The optics cleared the waves.

McKinnon quickly scanned the area for contacts. "Chief of the Watch, raise number two BRA-43," he ordered.

The dull green antenna and its gray, black spotted fairing slid above the surface.

"Conn, Radio, in sync with satellite," a voice announced.

"Very well, Radio," McKinnon replied. "Let me know if we receive any flash traffic."

"Conn, Radio, no new traffic. Request to copy 1600 news and sports."

"Not this time, Radio," McKinnon chuckled. "Chief of the Watch, lower all masts and antennas. All stations, Conn, going deep."

MIAMI angled back under the surface. She slowed to 7 knots, and steadied her depth at 400 feet.

"Sonar, deploy the arrays,"

From the edges of the vertical stabilizers, thin cables slowly paid out. Along the length of these cables small, but powerful passive transducers listened. Separated by hundreds of yards from the submarine, the arrays were free of even the smallest noise generated by their host.

When the arrays stabilized, USS MIAMI began her search.

"Conn, Sonar, what are we hunting for?" The Sonar Supervisor asked over the 27MC.

"Sonar, this is the Captain," McKinnon announced. "You will know when you hear it. Call out anything in the 27to 84 Hertz range."

The Sonar Supervisor could not hide the surprise in his voice. "Those are Russian frequencies."

"That's right, Sonar," McKinnon replied. He then turned to the Officer of the Deck. "Man Battle Stations."

SIMCER

Commander Feroz started his run toward New York Harbor just before noon.

A passing container ship provided cover for the first fifty miles. SIMCER followed in its wake until the faster ship outran the slower submarine.

Feroz checked the inertial navigation system. "Two knot current," he hissed. "We are in the Gulf Stream."

He moved to the battery monitor. The eight needles on the battery gauges hung like wilted flowers at just under half.

Feroz calculated his options. The batteries would require a half hour charge if he increased speed.

He went back to the chart. Soon, the ocean bottom would rise up to meet them. There would be nowhere to hide.

"Maneuvering control, increase speed to 6 knots," he rasped. "We will find cover after dark and charge the batteries. Sonar, find me a ship."

The Pentagon
Washington, DC

"Burke, we have a problem," Chairman of the Joint Chiefs of Staff Admiral Malroy muttered into the secure telephone.

Admiral Tarrent listened on his own secure line. "What now?"

"The President's flying to New York City."

"Mother of God, what for?" Tarrent barked.

"Fund-raisers." Malroy replyed. "Two days."

"Can you stop it?" Tarrent asked hopefully.

"In an election year?" Malroy snorted and continued. "That's not the worst of it."

"What could be worse?" Tarrent growled.

"The Vice President is at the UN summit on Asian economic growth. And just to top it off, the Speaker of the House is en route to

Elizabeth, New Jersey."

"Now, *that* is a problem," Tarrent grunted. "We're not sure New York is even a target. We don't know if it's a WMD. What we know , Jim, is squat!"

"I agree, old friend, but how many times have you and I played poker together? I'm telling you the Iranians wouldn't go to all this trouble to hit a few ships, or even launch a conventional cruise missile attack. As for a target... I know what I'd hit if it were me."

"Washington?" Tarrent asked.

"Not this time." Malroy responded in his deep Texas drawl. "They want the President to look like a jackass. You wipe out DC, and certain things will happen, automatically, if you get my drift. Don't think they want that."

"Okay, Jim," Tarrent took the bait. "What do *you* think they want?"

"I have no idea!" Malroy shot back. "But I'll try to come up with something to get the President to change his schedule. The Veep's locked into this summit. The Speaker's mother is on her death bed, so I won't be able to budge her." He paused before asking, "Heard anything from McKinnon?"

"Not yet," Tarrent rumbled. "Jim, this is getting dangerous!"

"Don't I know it!" Malroy snorted. "It's occurring to me that I'm getting too old for this."

"Me too."

Chapter Twenty-Four

FRIEND OR FOE

*"O poor mortals,
how ye make this earth
bitter for each other."*
~Thomas Carlyle,
The French Revolution,
Vol. I, Book II, Chapter 1

K-157 VEPR
January 17th

200-nautical miles from the mouth of New York Harbor, the Russian AKULA slowed. As her speed dropped, she shuddered slightly like a distance runner might after a marathon. As important as her speed had been, stealth was now her greatest asset.

She moved in the quiet darkness, just inside the Continental Shelf. It was not only a rogue KILO she needed to find, she herself had to remain unheard. This was the front yard of the American's Atlantic submarine fleet.

"Trail the towed array," Captain First Rank Danyankov ordered in a whisper. "Set quiet condition four."

He hoped only one American knew he was here. It would waste precious time to clear his baffles. He would keep VEPR quiet and steady.

Then it seemed his luck ran out.

"New sonar contact," the Sonar Officer announced. Then his voice suddenly became panicked "Submerged contact, close aboard!"

"Bearing?" Danyankov hissed.

"Bearing 200 drawing right!" The voice cracked as if its owner had just hit puberty.

The picture formed instantly in Danyankov's mind. An American submarine blind to his presence was about to collide broadside.

"Flood center trim," he shouted.

As the water filled the trim tanks, the AKULA sank deeper. Danyankov fought the urge to order more speed.

"50 meters." The Sonar Officer reported.

"Right ten," Danyankov commanded. He hoped if a collision did occur he could decrease the angle and cause the submarines to glance off each another.

VEPR obeyed slowly. The rounded bow swung in a graceful arc to the west. Danyankov had just opened his mouth to order a full bell when the voice of the Sonar Officer came to his ears.

"Captain, we hear tanks blowing bearing 197. The American is surfacing."

"Hold on." Danyankov shouted.

The sound of water and air surrounded the double hull of the AKULA. Instinctively, men stared at the overhead of VEPR's interior as if the America submarine would crash through at any second.

"She is right on top of us," Danyankov whispered, then barked, "Stop descent!"

Now a beating, whooshing sound filled the Russian submarine. It grew louder until the very steel of the AKULA's hull vibrated.

"Keep going," Danyankov muttered to the American.

The sound reached a crescendo. VEPR rocked slightly as pressure waves formed by the screw of the American submarine washed over her. Then as quickly as it had come, the sound faded.

The next was a low rush of air as stressed lungs relaxed.

Danyankov bowed his head slightly as the sound tapered to silence.

"Captain," the Sonar Officer's nervous voice called out. "The American appeared out of nowhere. A gradient of eight degrees is off our port side."

I should have slowed sooner. Danyankov chided himself. *Not the crew's fault.* He had taken a calculated risk.

"These things happen," Danyankov said

with a hint of kindness in his voice. "Is the American turning?"

"Contact now classified as surfaced early model LOS ANGELES class nuclear submarine. Contact bears 040. She has not maneuvered."

"Do you think they heard us?" The Navigator asked quietly.

Danyankov stood and rubbed his neck. "No," he answered. "If she had, she would have never come that close. She was blinded by the same gradient. We just happened into her path. The American is on her way home." Danyankov wondered how convincing he sounded. He tried hard to convince himself. "Return to base course," he ordered.

USS MIAMI SSN 755

The silent minutes seemed like hours. MIAMI's electronic ears caught, analyzed, and processed every sound, every signal, even the slightest electrical impulse.

She moved in a slow arc above and below the thermal layers; each wider than the last. When the arc ended at twenty miles from the start, she reversed course and searched in an expanding series of arcs that formed a 100-mile U-shape.

For all the wonderful technology and expensive gadgets, Grant McKinnon knew a sub verses sub fight would be a close-in nasty affair. It was what he had trained for all his life.

This was the hard part, the waiting. The part where the nerve of a true submariner is tested.

MIAMI completed her second set of arcs. She angled up to stick her spherical array above the 3-degree gradient, when a faint ultrahigh frequency impulse struck the third hydrophone of the towed array.

"Conn, Sonar, gained new contact. 33 Hertz tonal, bearing 070. Possible submerged contact. Designate Sierra 54. Sending to class," the Sonar Supervisor advised.

In the Control Room and Attack Center, nerves tensed. Fire Control received the data and a plot began. In the center of the screen, the shape of a small submarine designated MIAMI. A red triangle with a small dot in the center was the unknown contact.

"Talk to me, Sonar," McKinnon urged.

"Conn, Sonar, 33 Hertz tonal classified as submerged Russian built diesel submarine. Be advised contact is intermittent. Last good bearing 071."

McKinnon took in a deep breath. "Helm, come right to new course 020. We'll come over a bit and let the array get a broadside look."

"Conn, Sonar, we now hold new passive broadband contact on the same bearing as Sierra 54. Designate contact as Sierra 55. Classified as a merchant making 75 turns on one five-bladed screw."

"Sonar, are 55 and 54 the same contact?" McKinnon asked.

258 D. Clayton Meadows

"Conn, Sonar, that's a negative," the Sonar Supervisor answered. "We now hold hits of blade tip cavitation from Sierra 54."

McKinnon formed the picture in his mind. The KILO is using the merchant as cover. *Smart boy.* This made an attack impossible. *If it were me, I'd hug that merchant.* No way would anyone shoot a torpedo. McKinnon began searching in his own bag of tricks.

SIMCER
97 Nautical Miles from New York City

The large slow container ship they had settled behind in the early hours, was the perfect cover.

Commander Asha Feroz closed to 800 meters before coming near enough to the surface to raise his snorkel mast. Two hours later the KILO's batteries were fully charged.

SIMCER easily matched the freighter's 6 knots, and near the surface, the current of the warm Gulf Stream was a knot or two weaker.

Feroz nudged SIMCER closer to the lumbering freighter. Safe in her wake, SIMCER would be invisible At least, that is what Feroz thought.

Oval Office
The White House
Washington, DC

"Oh, come on, Jim!" The President of the United States jiggled something in his pants pocket and frowned at the Chairman of the Joint Chiefs. "I miss these fund raisers and there goes the Jewish vote."

"I understand, Mr. President," Admiral Malroy replied. "But I think a surprise visit to the troops in Korea would gain you a ton more votes. Not to mention sending that half-pint Hitler in the North a message. After all, you *have* visited the troops everywhere else."

The President looked puzzled. "I'm also campaigning for Senator Byron. You know, the Senate Armed Services Chair? We lose him and Elrick gets the seat, we'll go from tanks to bio-fueled go-carts in five years. Not to mention having "green" guns!"

"The visit would look good with the Veep's proposal for aid to Asia," Malroy pressed on.

The President walked to the windows, his back to Malroy. "It might, but I've got too much to worry about here at home."

"Will you at least consider it?"

"No can do, Jim. Sorry, but the stakes are just too high."

If you only knew! Malroy thought, defeated.

Chapter Twenty-Five

OLD FRIENDS

*"When a man does not know
what harbor he is making for,
no wind is the right wind."*
~Seneca

USS MIAMI SSN 755
January 17th

"XO," Commander Grant McKinnon whispered. "A word, please."

Lieutenant Commander Gellor followed McKinnon as he stepped into his stateroom.

"We have to spook this guy," McKinnon said, closing the door.

"Skipper, you do that and he might come out shooting," Gellor sighed. "By the time we evade his incoming, and set up for an attack, we might lose him. Then, what about that merchant?"

McKinnon bit his thumb. "What we need is a way to spook him without him knowing we're on to him."

Gellor's eyes narrowed "Okay, sir, you've got my attention."

McKinnon lifted his finger in the air. "What if we come to periscope depth and contact the merchant? Feed him some cock-and-bull story, anything to make him stop, or change course."

"I don't know," Gellor winced "We could lose him on the way up or he might hear us. For all we know, he might have a mast up, and is already listening. You go out clear voice and he'll know the jig's up."

McKinnon shook his head. "Never thought of that."

"Hey, er sir," Gellor perked up. "What if we sent up a radio slot buoy? Program a message to the Admiral? Have him contact the Coast Guard? Let 'em do the dirty work."

A sparkle gleamed in McKinnon's eyes. "Brad, I'm sure glad you're here." He started to grin, "Get it done!"

Ten minutes later, the radio message was uploaded to the buoy. McKinnon brought MIAMI gently to 80 feet. To avoid the noise of the 3-inch signal ejector, McKinnon ordered the buoy hand-rammed from the ejector tube.

Shoved out, the thin three foot long anodized steel cylinder sped upwards. Ten feet below the surface a spring-operated valve overcame sea pressure and opened a tiny hole.

Seawater flooded in and activated the buoy's internal batteries.

At the surface, a tiny electric explosive squib detonated. The small explosion, not much bigger than a cap gun, released the thin banding wire that held the buoy's three-foot antenna. A switch inside sensed the antenna was up. The batteries now powered a transmitter that beamed an encoded signal to a satellite. The short message broadcast five times.

After that, another pulse fired a larger electro-explosive. The gases from this explosion sent a superheated wave through the internal works of the buoy destroying the transmitter and the message playback card. The force of the gasses also blew out perforated plugs in the buoy's top and bottom. Water rushed in and filled the void. Now dead and useless, the buoy sank 850 feet to the bottom.

In MIAMI's Control Room, Commander McKinnon checked his watch. "I'll give it an hour," he nodded to the XO.

"Then what?" Gellor persisted.

McKinnon's eyes locked onto Gellor. "The merchant is in the wrong place at the wrong time."

Gellor's eyes fluttered suddenly as the meaning of McKinnon's words registered. "I hope the Admiral's at work."

"I hope..."

McKinnon was cut off by the voice of the

Sonar Supervisor. "Conn, Sonar, 127 Hertz Tonal on the towed array bearing 100 on the right drawing right. Designate 127 Hertz tonal as Sierra 56." There was a pause. "Conn, Sonar, this is a submerged contact. We are getting hits of steam flow."

"Can you classify?" McKinnon demanded.

"Conn, Sonar!" There was now some alarm in the Sonar Supervisor's voice, "Classified as late model Russian type 2-3 nuclear submarine." Again, there was a pause. "Captain, tonal information and broadband steam flow classify as..."

"What?" McKinnon urged.

"It's the VEPR. Captain."

Gellor cleared his throat. "You think she knows we're here?"

McKinnon held on to the low rail around the periscope stand. "Of course he does." He snorted a laugh. "Why do you think we heard him? He's letting us know he's here."

Gellor leaned close to McKinnon. "Skipper, you'd better let the guys know what's going on. There are now two Russian-built submarines inside our waters only 80 miles from New York, and the crew doesn't have a clue."

McKinnon pondered that. Telling the crew their families were in danger might help. It would answer the why of it. On the other hand, it might cause someone to do something stupid. "Okay, Brad, you tell Sonar what's going on. I'll take care of Control and the tracking party."

"What do you think our old friend out there has up his sleeve?" Gellor asked as he stepped off the periscope stand.

McKinnon shook his head. "Wish I knew."

"Bet he's had the same idea as us. That freighter's expendable." Gellor headed off to the Sonar shack.

* * *

MIAMI's encrypted message reached the satellite nine seconds after the buoy's first transmission.

Once received, the garble of digital 1s and 0s was analyzed by software inside the satellite's solar powered computer.

The software detected the correct sequence of number combinations and determined the message to be authentic.

Nanoseconds later, the message fed into another section of the electronic brain. Here the message's urgency and addressee were determined.

As on an assembly line, the message passed on to yet another section of the communication satellite. Here, it received a further encryption, and was then placed in the transmission queue.

Due to the urgency and the addressee, McKinnon's message left the satellite's antenna a mere three seconds later.

K-157 VEPR

"Sonar, has the American maneuvered?" Captain First Rank Valerik Danyankov barked.

"No sir. Contact maintains a constant bearing," the Sonar Officer replied.

"Do you think he heard us?" The Navigator asked quietly.

"I'm making more noise than a freight train!" Danyankov hissed. "The Persian?"

"Iranian submarine bears 358. Range steady at 1100 meters."

Danyankov's instinct was to kill the submarine, now. He was in a perfect firing position. One torpedo would do it. An easy shot except for the container ship, and the American submarine.

If not for that rust bucket up there, Danyankov thought, *McKinnon would have already killed the Persian.*

Other than sending torpedoes toward the KILO, his own options were limited. He had to do what he hated most. Trust that McKinnon knew what he was doing.

Danyankov stepped to the digital chart. A thin computer-generated line marked the AKULA's course. 112 kilometers to New York. *McKinnon, my friend, I hope you have an idea very soon.* He watched the line flicker toward the harbor.

Now a green line appeared on the chart. This one designated the Persian. It snaked close to a set of black dots that denoted the course and speed of the bulk freighter.

Then another line, this time blue, flickered on the screen. This was McKinnon's MIAMI.

Danyankov stared at the red line. He suddenly imagined his father staring down at a paper chart. *He had been here on this very spot. Is this the course you took?* Memories again flooded his mind. The tin toy submarine his father gave him. The smile on his father's tired face when. at last, he would step off the submarine and they could walk home to their home on the third floor of the Officers' Billet.

A new image slipped into his mind. He saw himself as he stepped off VEPR's bow. Evelina would be there in her best dress. Next to her, a fidgety boy would stop kicking the snow and stare in awe as the sleek submarine slid alongside the pier.

His vision ended as the Sonar Officer's voice rang in his ear.

"Captain, we just picked up a faint American fathometer on the same bearing as the MIAMI."

"So he does know we are here," Danyankov answered dryly. "Did the Persian react?"

"No sir, she maintains 6 knots constant bearing and range," the Sonar Officer responded.

"Good," Danyankov nodded. "Tucked under the freighter, she is nearly deaf."

SIMCER

Wash from the container ship's propeller caused the small submarine to roll gently in rhythm with the beat of the water above. Blanked out by the turbulence of the freighter's wake, SIMCER's MGK-400 Rubikon passive sonar was nearly useless. High frequency signals could still be detected, but only if they originated no more than a few kilometers away.

Satisfied with SIMCER's position, Commander Feroz stepped from the command center to his small cabin.

From his pant's pocket, he took out a key. He slid it into the slot of his wall locker. The hinged door swung open.

Feroz stared at the device. It was the same shape and not much larger than a child's lunch box.

A neatly coiled braided coaxial cable fed from near the top. At its end hung a plug, not unlike a USB port plug, wrapped in protective pink film.

On the face of the device, a row of three green-colored lenses stared out blank and dull. Below these, two simple switches poked from the box's interior. Set in a vertical row the upper switch carried the label ACTIVATE. Below it, another was marked POWER.

On the bottom of the box, a heavy-duty cord like those used on vacuum cleaners coiled in neat loops, around a bracket of hard black plastic.

Feroz turned it gently in his hands. "Power," he whispered to himself.

106th Air Rescue Wing
New York Air National Guard
Westhampton Beach, New York

Major Samson Dellerino – call sign Butch – said little as he climbed into the seat of his HH-60 PAVE HAWK helicopter, SANDY-1.

Next to him, twenty-three year old co-pilot First Lieutenant Coit Cox – call sign CC – was not so quiet.

"If this isn't a rescue, what is it?" Cox asked as he switched the radio to the proper frequency.

"Don't know," Dellerino replied with a shrug. "Clear," he shouted as the powerful twin turbofan engines of the PAVE HAWK began to whine.

Cox switched on the interior comm system. "Come on, Major, spill it!" He urged.

Now the rotor blades thrashed at the sky. Dellerino checked the gauges and warning lights. "I'm telling you, Loot, that's all I know. The Colonel got some call from DC, and here we are."

Cox shook his head. "Weird."

Dellerino keyed his microphone. "Tower, this is SANDY-1. Lifting off." He pulled gently on the collective and the HH-60 lifted into the air.

At 150 feet, Dellerino applied pressure on the right rudder pedal. The powerful helicopter obeyed, and swung her nose toward the sea.

Chapter Twenty-Six

DOGFIGHT

"Remember
upon the conduct of each
depends the fate of all."
~Alexander the Great

50 Nautical Miles From New York City
USS MIAMI SSN 755

In MIAMI's Attack Center, Executive Officer Lieutenant Commander Gellor checked his watch. "Almost an hour," he said quietly. "Water's getting mighty shallow."

Commander Grant McKinnon nodded. "Sonar, Conn, anything new from the contacts?"

"Conn, Sonar, negative."

McKinnon closed his eyes. His brain formed a picture of the KILO, the VEPR, and the freighter. Something scratched at his brain as if asking to be let in. *I'm forgetting something.* For a few short seconds, he tried to remember what. Then a voice over the 27MC chased away any thoughts.

"Conn, Sonar, I'm picking up slight surface disturbance bearing 020. New contact is a passive broadband on the sphere. Bottom bounce range is 30,000 yard with a slight closure. Classify as a helo."

"Looks like the Admiral opened his mail after all," Gellor grinned.

"Maybe," McKinnon rubbed his chin.

"Thirty-K will put him beyond visual,"

"Sonar, where's the chopper now?" McKinnon asked.

"Conn, Sonar, seems to be hovering. Range remains constant."

The XO looked at McKinnon. "Any ideas?"

"Maybe," MIAMI's Captain replied. "Fire Control, silent flood tubes one through four."

HH-60 PAVE HAWK
SANDY-1

First Lieutenant Coit Cox looked down into the greenish glow of the helicopter's AN/APR-39(V)2 radar receiver. "Major, I have a lock on the freighter," He announced over the thumping whine of the helicopter's engines.

"Roger that," Major Dellerino acknowledged. "Keep me just beyond visual range, and patch me in on ship-to-ship."

The co-pilot adjusted the radio set. "Okay, you're patched in."

Dellerino keyed the microphone. "Unknown vessel, this is United States Army helicopter off your bow. You are ordered to stop immediately. Do you copy?"

Cox looked up from the radar receiver. "What?"

Dellerino seemed not to hear. Again, he pressed the mic key. "Unknown vessel, I say again, do you copy? I have authorization to fire upon you if you do not halt."

There was a burst of static, then a voice of definite Scandinavian origin came into the Dellerino's headset. "This is Danish ship, *Ailsa Kirkegard*, bound for New York. We are cleared by your US Coast Guard to enter harbor."

"*Ailsa Kirkegard*, this is US Army helicopter. Clearance to enter Port of New York cancelled. Stop now or be fired upon."

"She's slowing," Cox said nervously.

"Tell me when she's dead in the water," Dellerino ordered.

SIMCER

"Captain!" A frantic voice called over the ship wide public address system. "The surface ship has slowed. Her screw has stopped."

In seconds, Feroz was in the command center. "Ahead full! Right rudder," he rasped.

Slow, but nimble, the Russian built KILO

answered the helm. She swung right as her five bladed screw dug into the water.

"Continue right," Feroz ordered. "We are too close to the ship."

SIMCER continued her turn. As the wash of the freighter's screw died off, the KILO's passive sonar could now hear.

"Unknown submerged contact bearing 023 range 316 meters," the Sonar Officer called out.

"How?" Feroz rasped in fury. "Reaction fire along the bearing," he barked as his submarine turned toward the unknown contact.

For a small submarine, SIMCER packed quite an arsenal. In her bow rested six forward firing 533mm torpedo tubes. A computer driven system that required no human interaction could reload each tube in three minutes.

The bearing and range automatically fed from the MGK-400 Sonar to the fire control data computer. The electronic information passed to the guidance system in the ETS-80 torpedoes. Within seconds, three of the six torpedoes had the required information.

On the KILO's attack console, three amber lights changed green. "Ready to launch," the Weapons Officer called out.

"Fire!" Feroz ordered.

In the KILO's torpedo room, vent and flood valves rolled open. Pressurized seawater quickly surrounded the waiting torpedoes.

When sensors registered a zero differential between pressure in the tubes and outside sea pressure, hydraulic actuators opened the outer torpedo tube doors.

HH-60 PAVE HAWK
SANDY-1

"She's stopped," Lieutenant Cox announced.

Major Dellerino nodded. "*Ailsa Kirkegard*, this is U. S. Army helicopter off your bow. You are to remain stopped until further notice. How copy?"

"This is *Ailsa Kirkegard*. Understand we are to remain stopped. We will file protest," the ship's Master radioed back.

Dellerino showed some teeth. "Roger that." He pushed the right rudder peddle. The HH-60 spun until its nose pointed west. "Okay kid, we're outta here."

"Say again?" Cox asked in amazement.

"Mission complete," Dellerino said as he pushed the throttle forward.

"What was the mission?" Cox yelled over the scream of the two-turbofan engines.

Dellerino grinned again. "No idea!"

K-157 VEPR

Captain First Rank Danyankov had seconds to make the correct decision.

Though the sudden stop of the freighter caught him off guard, he knew what was going to happen next.

A turn to the left would put MIAMI in the path of the torpedoes he knew were coming.

He could not turn right. The AKULA was slow and a turn would rob him of forward momentum. A right turn would also give the torpedoes a large surface area to home on. VEPR's only hope was to close the range, snuggle up to the Persian, and let the torpedoes go by. *If it was a bearing-only shot, I can evade.*

"Ahead flank," Danyankov shouted. He thought of alerting MIAMI to the threat, but decided to draw the fire and keep McKinnon unknown. *Here is your chance!* He felt VEPR's powerful screw chew into the water.

SIMCER

Timed at three second intervals, the three 6.3-meter-long weapons exited the KILO's bow. Instantly, their high capacity batteries fed raw amperage to the torpedoes motors. With the sound of a well-tuned chainsaws, each weapon headed along its preset gyro angle.

"Continue the turn," Commander Feroz rasped. "Down to 20 meters, steady on base course."

"Captain, charted depth is the 62 meters," the Diving Officer warned.

"We cannot maintain this speed for long," the new Engineer objected nervously.

"Mark distance to the harbor,"   T h e Navigator leaned over the chart. "80-

kilometers," he reported.

"Connect the device to the active system," Feroz barked. *We only have to stay alive for 20 kilometers.*

USS MIAMI SSN 755

"**Conn, Sonar, torpedoes** in the water!" Cried the Sonar Supervisor. "We now hold three inbound weapons bearing 177, 170, and 165."

Commander McKinnon could feel the nerve of each man tighten. "That's behind us," McKinnon announced. "Stay cool everyone, the KILO's shooting at VEPR."

"VEPR has increased speed. We hold massive cavitation on her last good bearing," Sonar reported. "We hold increased flow noise from the KILO."

"Fire Control, set it up! Give me a solution. If VEPR turns out of the way, I want an ADCAP on that KILO," McKinnon ordered.

"Conn, Sonar," the Sonar Supervisor called out. "Torpedo bearing 154 has gone active."

"What?" McKinnon exclaimed. "It's not had that long to run!"

"We're picking up reverb from the torpedo, wait... torpedo has acquired VEPR."

McKinnon looked at the waterfall display mounted just above eye level. He could see the line that marked the Russian AKULA. "Come on," McKinnon hissed. He watched as the line that marked the torpedo track steadily toward

Danyankov's submarine.

"Where are the other two weapons?" McKinnon calmly asked.

"Conn, Sonar, torpedoes passed astern now bearing 188 and 194, increasing range."

McKinnon looked at the picture on the waterfall display. VEPR had come up to almost 22 knots but the 43-knot weapon steadily closed the distance. McKinnon's eye found as small glimmer of hope. "Sonar, what's the DIMUS trace in the lower DE?"

"Believe this to be bottom bounce, 124 Hertz." Sonar reported.

McKinnon felt his heart sink and his mind race as the torpedo steadily tracked toward VEPR. "Why doesn't he maneuver?"

"Solution set," Fire Control announced.

"Snap-shot tube two," McKinnon ordered.

"Ship ready," announced the Diving Officer.

"Stand by," MIAMI's Weapons Officer called out. There was a half-second delay as the final settings for the ADCAP torpedo downloaded into the weapons electronic brain.

Then the weapon ready green light came on. "Shoot!" The Weapons Officer announced and the Fire Control technician moved the actuating lever from STAND BY to FIRE.

MIAMI shuddered slightly as 3000-pounds of compressed air drove a water piston to force the one-ton weapon into the waiting sea.

"Conn, Sonar, we hold motor start."

"He'll know we're here now," Gellor

muttered. "He could swing round and pop a shot off at us."

McKinnon's eyes went again to the passive waterfall display. His own torpedo almost blanked the screen as the sound of the ADCAP's six-cylinder external combustion engine filled the surrounding water.

He had done all he could. His trained eye picked out the Iranian torpedo as it merged with the trace that marked VEPR. This time a large green ball flashed across the screen. It then seemed to expand in all directions. McKinnon knew what it meant even as Sonar reported.

"Conn, Sonar, loud explosion on the last good bearing for VEPR." There was a pause. "Conn, Sonar, VEPR is gone."

McKinnon felt a lump form at the back of his throat. *Time for that later.*

"Conn, Sonar, the KILO just launched a decoy bearing 354."

"Where's our weapon?" McKinnon asked.

* * *

2000 yards from MIAMI, the ADCAP torpedo scanned for her prey. Transducers in the rubber-coated nose pinged out, while others listened for an echo.

A return struck the nose and the microprocessor evaluated the quality. The echo barely met the programmed criteria for a valid target but the torpedo turned to follow. It pinged again hungry for more information. A blast of noise blanked the return echo.

The passive receivers tried to filter the useless noise but the intensity caused the logic circuit to reset. A memory card activated and steered the torpedo toward the last good echo.

It pinged again. Now multiple returns entered the microprocessor, none of them valid. Another circuit switched on and the torpedo turned again toward the place in the ocean where the target should be if it maintained course and speed. Again, nothing registered.

This time the program directed a turn in the opposite direction. The 40-knot torpedo gracefully turned and pinged. Only cloudy returns from the bottom, and these were filtered out.

Now it dove to120 feet. The torpedo sensed a change in water temperature. It pinged again, and caught a faint return just off the right side. It made a slight course change and pinged. This time the return was better.

The weapon increased speed. Three seconds later another ultrasonic wave of sound left the nose. Again the echo disappeared. The weapon understood that the target had climbed above the thermal layer.

The computer adjusted the control surfaces to give the weapon a slight upward climb above the temperature gradient. The acoustic nose of the ADCAP pitched up to pursue, and ran out of fuel.

USS MIAMI SSN 755

"Weapon has shutdown," the Sonar Chief called out.

"McKinnon shook his head. "Sonar, where is the KILO?"

"Conn, Sonar, we've lost it."

Chapter Twenty-Seven

PULSES

*"There is no fate
but your own fate."*
~Leslie Grimutter

USS MIAMI SSN 755

This guy's good! A sliver of fear crawled up Commander Grant McKinnon's legs. It wound its way through his chest and slithered inside his head.

"Maybe he bottomed," Executive Officer Lieutenant Commander Gellor commented.

"Don't think so," McKinnon countered. "Distance to land?"

"34 miles," the Navigator answered. "Captain, charted water depth will be 40 fathoms if we stay on this course."

McKinnon's mind recalled the underwater topography of the area. "Bearing to deep water?"

The Navigator ran his finger over the chart. "80 fathoms bearing 358," he responded.

McKinnon pictured the sea floor. Set in a shallow upward incline, the bottom resembled the face of the moon. Rather than rises and hills, this part of the seabed featured craters and depressions, some close, some miles apart.

A random thought tickled at his brain, *Forgot to look up!* He remembered the briefing report he'd read. "Dive, make your depth 75 feet," he ordered. "Helm, left full rudder steady course 350."

Gellor looked puzzled. "Where are we going, Skipper?"

"We'll head over to some deeper water, run ahead, and then float near the top." McKinnon nodded. "We might get a sniff of him."

SIMCER
36 Nautical Miles from New York City

The KILO moved at 8 knots as she hugged the bottom, her keel no more than 3 meters from the mud and rock of the sea floor.

Even in the cool chill of the KILO, sweat dripped down the nose and face of Commander Asha Feroz. He was minutes from fulfilling his mission. There might even be the chance of escape.

He had defeated one submarine and avoided the torpedo of another. Now it was time to activate the device.

"Thirty miles," he rasped. He moved the few steps to the active sonar control panel. The device sat ready, its cable plugged firmly into the sound generator module. Feroz ran his fingers along the cool gray steel. Gently he toggled the power switch.

A barely audible hum flowed from the box. On the face, the three lights flashed in a steady pulsing rhythm. Feroz looked at the active display. The system indicated full power. His active sonar could deliver an acoustic pulse whose output energy equaled that of a good-sized radio station.

USS MIAMI SSN755
29 Nautical Miles from New York City

"40 fathoms," the Navigator called out.

"Dive! Make your depth 56 feet. Helm, come right to course 020," McKinnon snapped. "Chief of the Watch to maneuvering, make turns for 3 knots."

"We're out of water," Gellor noted.

"XO get on number two scope," McKinnon said as he pointed to the silver barrel of the multi-purpose periscope. "We don't need anyone bumping into us."

"Raising number two scope," Gellor announced as he spun the orange scope-operating ring.

"Attention in Control," McKinnon stated.

"We'll hang here nice and quiet. When the KILO tries to pass under, we'll take her out. This is going to be close."

"No close contacts," Gellor said as he swung the scope in a quick circle. "I hold land on this bearing... mark."

"290," the Fire Control plot recorder answered.

"I hold the outline of the city at three divisions in high power," Gellor stated for the official record.

For the first time in an hour, McKinnon found the time to think. Once more, the fate of unsuspecting thousands, perhaps millions rested firmly on him. And once again, he was alone.

He looked at the television monitor, slaved to the optics of number two periscope. The outline of the city was clear. *Jennifer and Misty are only 108 miles north.* "XO, what's the weather like?"

"Say again?" Gellor reacted.

McKinnon's eyes narrowed. "Which way is the wind blowing?"

Gellor's eyes went wide with understanding. He placed his eye back into the rubber eyepiece and elevated the optics until they pointed skyward.

McKinnon saw Gellor's shoulders slump.

"Wind about 10 to 12 knots. High cirrus clouds, winds out of the south blowing north," Gellor's words trailed off to a hopeless hiss.

10 knots at the surface, probably 20 above 5,000 feet. McKinnon felt his blood grow hot. It would only take three, maybe four hours, for the radioactive fallout to reach Groton.

He could see the panic. The roads jammed with the cars that managed to start as they tried to flee the toxic cloud. There would be no phones, the electromagnetic pulse of the blast would kill all unshielded electronics. For most, there would be no place to go.

His mind pictured Misty. He saw her afraid, her sweet face now streamed with tears, as something invisible, something she did not understand, killed her.

"That's it!" McKinnon shouted angrily. "Sonar, line up to go active 0db," he barked. "If we have to, we'll ram."

"Lining up to go active," the Sonar Supervisor replied.

"XO, lower the scope. Chief of the Watch to maneuvering shift reactor coolant pumps to fast speed. Be ready for a flank bell."

SIMCER
31 Nautical Miles from New York City

Inexperience and fear caused the Sonar Officer not to notice the lack of noise just ahead of SIMCER's bow.

His ears, strained after an intense hour, could hear the sounds of fish, crabs and clicking shrimp. The noises bounced around his head until his brain ignored the obvious. 250 meters ahead and near the surface, the noises faded.

He listened to the area where his ears enjoyed the quiet, but he didn't understand the significance.

Commander Feroz knew the American submarine was out there. Where, he neither knew nor cared. It was too late now. He had done it. The mighty American Navy at last was defeated. A few more meters and revenge would be complete. Justice delivered on a grand scale.

With a deep breath of the cool thick air, Feroz stepped to the device, running his fingers lightly over the warm gray surface.

He smiled as he looked at the clock ticking away above the fire control computer. "One minute," he said to no one in particular.

New York City

Satellite News Today broke into its normal daytime line-up of talk shows to carry the President's address.

Anchorwoman Sandra Beevy informed viewers of the President's fund raisers, scheduled for later in the afternoon and about the next day's flight to Aspen, Colorado. She had barely finished before the President stepped to the microphone.

"Good afternoon, my fellow Americans." He smiled that trademark grimace of his. "I'd like to thank the Society for Historic Preservation for inviting me to share in their Centennial Anniversary.

"We hear a lot about history, but few are afforded the chance to share in what history really means to America.

"With the help of organizations such as this one, a great many Americans will now have the chance to see the same buildings, ships, and other artifacts that is our heritage..."

USS MIAMI SSN 755
45 Seconds

Grant McKinnon's face felt hot as his hunter's blood pumped through his veins. He had opened his mouth to order the high-powered active search, when Sonar called out.

"Conn, Sonar, threat contact on the sphere, passive broad and narrow band. Contact bearing 110, range by bottom bounce 1000 yards and closing."

"Got 'em!" McKinnon hissed.

"Too close for a shot," Gellor announced as he looked at the Fire Control solution.

"Ahead flank, cavitate!" McKinnon ordered. "We'll open range to 1500 yards. Helm left full rudder." His breath came in deep pants.

SIMCER
30 Seconds

"Captain! American submarine Los Angeles Class, bearing 0 range 900 meters," the Sonar Officer screamed.

Commander Feroz moved his finger to the ACTIVATE button.

"Captain, the American is turning away. He is opening range."

Feroz stared at the clock as if not hearing the desperate voice of the Sonar Officer.

"Captain—"

"I heard you," Feroz rasped as his eyes widened with each tick of the second hand.

New York City
15 Seconds

"I say to all Americans." the President continued, "to not only preserve history, but become part of history. Strive to accomplish great things. One way to do this is to educate our nation's children..."

USS MIAMI SSN 755
10 Seconds

"Speed is 16 knots," the Diving Officer reported as MIAMI swung around.

"Range 1-100 yards," Fire Control reported.

"Set it up," McKinnon ordered as he watched the MK-19 gyro repeater slowly rotate. "I want that weapon in the water when we steady."

SIMCER
5 Seconds

Commander Feroz's finger trembled as the last seconds ticked slowly away. He smiled as the small needle moved closer to his destiny and to his revenge.

New York City

"History," the President went on, "is not only building and things we can touch. History is people and places..."

SIMCER
Time 0

Commander Feroz hesitated for another half second. "Now!" He whispered and his finger gently nudged the ACTIVATE switch.

The device hummed louder and the active portion of SIMCER's sonar switched to high power.

Somewhere inside the device, relays shut with a loud click. The first green light illuminated as a wave of sound pulsed through the shallow sea.

The sound that left the KILO's bow mounted active system resembled the wail of a European type siren, a few octaves lower. The sound traveled along the gentle slope of the bottom, propagating the impulse to spread in a 20-

degree arc, just as designed.

Ellis Island

Weakened by only a fraction, the sound energy struck the long forgotten weapon.

The receivers sent the signal to the primitive processor, which verified it was indeed the correct frequency, and amplitude. The first reed switched closed. Voltage began to build in the firing capacitor.

USS MAIM SSN 755

"What was that?" McKinnon shouted.

"Conn, Sonar, unknown active transmission from the KILO."

"Range to target 1300 yards. Thirty seconds to a firing solution," the Weapons Officer reported.

"Something's not right, Skipper," Executive Officer Gellor huffed.

SIMCER

Like watching a child *being born*, Asha Feroz's eyes looked lovingly at the device, as its hum again grew loud.

"Power down to 60 percent," warned the new Engineer.

The second light illuminated a bright green as another wave of sound energy erupted from the KILO's stubby bow. This sound was a deep low rumbled of exactly proportioned waves that lasted 100 milliseconds.

Ellis Island

As this second wave of sound washed over the waiting weapon, the second of the three reed switches shut. A small motor turned a small gear train.

As the gears rotated, a slide arm moved a 6-millimeter plate of non-conductive hard rubber from between the firing contacts. The contacts once held apart by the hard rubber plate now meshed.

All that was needed was the final pulse to send the current built up in the capacitor.

USS MIAMI SSN 755

"Second active pulse from the KILO," Sonar reported.

"Ease the rudder to left 10 degrees," McKinnon ordered. MIAMI was ten seconds from launch point.

"Conn, Sonar," the Sonar Supervisor called out. "High bearing rate DIMUS, bearing 040. Torpedo in the water."

McKinnon blinked in amazement. "040?"

"Conn, Sonar, it's not from the KILO."

"Left hard rudder," McKinnon shouted. He grabbed the 1MC microphone and shouted.

"Maneuvering, Conn, open the throttle."

"Conn, Sonar, torpedo has gone active, now bearing 050 on the right drawing left. Captain," the Sonar Supervisor's excited voice reported, "it's locked on the KILO."

"How?" McKinnon bellowed.

MIAMI's seven bladed screw churned as it sought traction in the water that swirled around it.

"Brace!"The Sonar Supervisor shouted over the 27MC. "This is going to be close."

SIMCER

Commander Feroz listened as the device hummed for the third time. It was then that he noticed another louder hum from somewhere outside the hull.

He turned his head to the Sonar Officer who sat rigid, his eyes wide, silent mouth dropped open.

* * *

At 45 knots, the two-ton weapon burrowed through the lighter steel of the small submarine's outer hull.

Inside the warhead, an inertial ball switch sensed the sudden deceleration and detonated the half ton of high explosive.

The explosion tore the small submarine in two sections. A ten-foot ball of plasma and steam shot through the ends of the two sections, melting and burning through steel as if it were water.

Pressure from the ocean rushed back to fill the void and smashed into notepaper sized sheets and globs of twisted scrap, what bits of the submarine were left.

* * *

It happened in a hundredth of a second. However, before the heat of the explosion incinerated him, Asha Feroz saw the green lights of the device flutter and blink out.

New York City

"As long as there are Americans willing to carry the torch, our history will continue.

"In the future, what we do here today will be remembered. I salute the Historical Preservation Society. I am sure your next hundred years will be even better than the last. Thank you."

The television feed changed back to Anchorwoman Sandra Beevy. "In summary, the President talked about the importance of historical preservation. I will have more at the top of the hour. Now let's return you to Janet Burnstein's special, CITY BLOOMS. Janet will show New Yorkers how they can make some beautiful things grow with a little space and know-how."

Chapter Twenty Eight

THE OBVIOUS

*"The obscure we see eventually.
The completely obvious, it seems,
takes longer."*
~Edward R. Murrow

USS MIAMI SSN 755

With her stern to the explosion, the American submarine felt little as the waves of pressure flowed around her. The raw energy of the blast subsided quickly and MIAMI steadied.

"Ahead one-third," Commander Grant McKinnon ordered.

"What happened?" Executive Officer Gellor asked, as he blotted sweat from his brow with his sleeve.

McKinnon could only shake his head. "I don't know."

Gellor lifted his finger in the air. "Maybe it

was..."

His words were cut off by a noise that seemed to enter the Control Room and echo off the insulated steel of MIAMI's hull.

McKinnon heard the Sonar Supervisor screech in pain, then curse. "Conn, Sonar, received active transmission in the baffles bearing 200. Active classified as SHARKGILL Mod. 2." Then the voice became excited, "Captain, only one Russian submarine carries that sonar suite. Sir, it's the VEPR."

"How?" The XO asked. "We saw him die."

"You forget," McKinnon smiled. "It's Danyankov. Sonar, line up on the bottom transducer for the WQC-2."

When the speaker for the underwater voice system was switched on, a wavy static filled the MIAMI's Control Room. Then a voice came through the noise, "Yankee-1, Yankee-1, this is Gray Ghost."

Grant McKinnon felt a lump come back into his throat. He snatched the underwater communicator's handset and pressed the button. "Gray Ghost, this is Yankee-1, we thought you were dead." He said as a tear streaked down his face.

"Yankee-1, certainly not me." Danyankov sounded insulted. "My MG-74 took the hit."

"MG-74?" The Navigator asked.

"MG-74 Korund," the Sonar Supervisor answered. "It's like our MOSS simulator. It takes a recording of the firing ship's noise signature, packs it into a torpedo-like shape and shoots it off. Once in the water, it transmits the noise."

"VEPR must have been that faint 124 Hertz we saw," McKinnon noted.

Then the voice came again, "Yankee 1, this is Gray Ghost. We need to talk."

"Roger that," McKinnon answered. "When?"

"Three weeks. I have another mission. This is Gray Ghost... out."

McKinnon wondered about that "other mission" as he hung up the handset.

"Officer of the Deck," McKinnon at last relaxed. "Secure from battle stations, and point us for home."

Tehran, Iran
January 19th

The wait had worn on Iranian President Mehran's nerves. He had been shut up in this room with the old cleric most of the day. He had been offered no food, no drink. It was just him, the Koran and the Supreme Ayatollah Majeed Ali Sohrab.

To relieve his cramped legs he'd begun pacing back and forth beside the door.

Toward evening, when the call to prayers was heard from the city mosques, the old man finally spoke, "There is no news of disaster from America."

Mehran's throat went dry. He was unable to

say a word. Not that any would have helped.

"We must assume that once again your plans have failed," Sohrab whispered. He picked up his cell phone and pressed a key. When nothing happened, he peered at it and gave it a shake.

Mehran shrank back into a corner of the room when he heard heavy footsteps stop outside the door.

The old cleric, unaware, kept pressing buttons on his phone, then held it to his ear.

When the door crashed open, three men clad in Iranian army fatigues burst in, armed with AK-47s.

Only then did the old man slowly move around on the cushions. "And who are you?"

The tallest of the three sneered down at the cleric. "We bring a message from the Americans," he barked as he thrust a sheet of paper at the Ayatollah.

He took it in his shaking claw.

Printed in English in capital letters big enough for Mehran to read from across the room, the short message said: WE KNOW.

The old man's dark eyes popped. For the first time Mehran saw an emotion register on Ayatollah Majeed Ali Sohrab's withered face. And it was fear.

The three intruders backed up and leveled their weapons at the seated cleric.

Mehran clapped his hands over his ears as the gunfire clattered and blinding flashes reflected like the fires of hell off the blood splattered walls.

The old Ayatollah's bullet-riddled body keeled over as pools of blood seeped out from his robes cascading over the cushions.

"The people like you, President Mehran." A voice said as the echo of the machine guns died away "Can you make peace with the Americans?"

Mehran lifted his head, straightened his back. "I think so," he said feebly.

"Then, you will do it," the leader of the three men hissed. "And remain President until the next general election."

"After that?" Mehran stuttered.

The man swung the barrel of his AK-47 toward the dead cleric. "That depends on the quality of your peace," he replied. "Now, Mr. President, come with us."

Naval Submarine Base
Groton, Connecticut
January, 20th

MIAMI passed up the Thames River mostly unnoticed. Her sleek hull, sliding silently through the cold waters, garnered few a glances from the tourists who had braved the chill of the clear, cold day to visit the NAUTILUS SSN 571 museum. Those that did, waved to the passing submarine from behind the glass walls.

Grant McKinnon stood in the sail. Cold or

not, it was a beautiful day.

He looked over at his home base. Sailors and civilians, workers and visitors, all went about their business. He smiled for them. It could have been a very different Friday afternoon.

In that moment, Commander Grant McKinnon felt once more, what life and being alive meant. He wanted to laugh, to shout.

Then another thought, one that had tugged at him for days, now pounded at his skull. He felt a shiver start from his feet until it tingled at the top of his head. *No guts, no glory."*

The tugs met MIAMI just south of the base. They quickly latched on with their three inch thick hawsers, and nudged the 360-foot submarine into her allotted berth. Soon, the lines were fast to the bollards.

With the ship secured, wives, girlfriends, mothers, fathers, sons and daughters streamed down the narrow pier. Their sailors met them with hugs and kisses unlike they had known.

MIAMI had not been at sea that long, and the emotional greetings caught a few of the ladies off-guard.

Officers and enlisted alike held their children a little longer, and clutched their wives, as if it were for the first time.

Only the crew of MIAMI knew what might have been.

Their Commanding Officer stood at the end of the bow as McKinnon stepped off. The two saluted.

"That was a close one," Tarrent sighed.

"Yes sir," McKinnon answered as he strode past the Admiral.

"Grant?" Tarrent turned in pursuit. "We need to debrief."

"Tomorrow, sir" McKinnon called over his shoulder.

He spotted her standing next to the blue plastic guard shack.

Misty saw him at the same time and began jumping up and down as she pointed.

Tarrent still had some bounce in him despite his age, and he managed to catch up to within ten yards of McKinnon, when he saw him reach for Jennifer, and they melted together in a deep kiss.

"Hey, what about me?" Misty shrilled as she tugged on his jacket

McKinnon scooped her into his arms.

"What's wrong?" Jennifer asked. "You look terrible."

Tarrent, still on a full head of steam, was now only five yards away.

"Will you marry me?" McKinnon blurted out, louder than he planned.

Tarrent stopped dead in his tracks, his mouth as if on a broken hinge, swung open.

Jennifer's eyes doubled in size. She tried to form words, but none came.

Misty sighed, reached out and placed her small hand under her mother's chin. "Just say yes, Mommy."

Tears sprang into Jennifer's eyes. She took a gulp of air. "Yes!" She laughed.

"Tomorrow'll be just fine," Admiral Tarrent called out as he veered off to his waiting car.

The White House
Washington, DC

"Jim," the President said warmly, "can you believe the Iranians? They just gave up." He clapped his hands together. "Mehran wants to open embassies. Here in "Satan's" land. The man's going to Israel... Israel!" He shook his head as if he couldn't believe it.

Chairman of the Joint Chiefs of Staff, Admiral Malroy smiled thinly. "Yes, Mr. Present, that is good news."

The President's smile dropped from his face. "What is it, Jim? You don't seem very... happy about it."

"Mr. President," Malroy said as he reached into his briefcase, "I want to tell you a story. After that, I want you to sign these." He handed over a folder.

"What is it?" The President asked.

"My request to retire."

Satellite News Today
January 23rd
4:32 AM

Anchorman Gary O'Dannon broke in on the rerun of a piece about a 90 year old woman running for mayor of a small town in Iowa.

"We'll get back to Mrs. Harris's bid for office" he said, putting on his serious face, "but we have breaking news.

According to the wire resources, an Iranian supertanker , the *Behzad Nabavi*... hope I said that right... has exploded and sunk in the Atlantic Ocean some 400 miles off South America. According to Iranian sources, the ship was empty.

Search teams from three Latin American nations have found no survivors. And now," O'Dannon gave the camera his trademark perky smile. "What's ahead for your weekend weather when we return."

Chapter Twenty-Nine

WORDS

"One's suffering disappears
when one lets oneself go,
when one yields even to sadness."
~Antoine de Saint-Exupéry,
Southern Mail, 1929,
translated from French by Curtis Cate

Seven Months Later

Some 4,000 miles apart, two men walked with their families along rows of tenderly cared for memorial stones until each reached the ones they sought.

In Russia and America, warm summer breezes wafted the scents of pine trees and flowers over the serene, sacred places.

Both men trod slowly, uncomfortable as they faced their pasts etched in marble and stone. Each man took in deep breaths of the fragrant air. Each knew their visit to these places was necessary.

In Severodvinsk, Russia, Valerik Danyankov, with Evelina at his side and their son, Yuri Grant in his arms, faced a gravestone of polished black granite. Neatly etched in the gleaming surface were the words:

CAPTAIN FIRST RANK
MIKHAIL DANYANKOV
1943—1970
HERO OF THE SOVIET UNION

Evelina took the baby from her husband's arms as he stepped forward, saluted his father's grave and then bowed his head.

"Poppa," he whispered, "I never understood why I should come here, until today. I present to you my wife and your grandson. I wish you to be proud of what I have done with the life you gave me."

* * *

In Noank, Connecticut, Grant and Jennifer McKinnon, with Misty between them, stood before the side-by-side graves set on a small grassy hill over looking the sea.

Misty stepped up to the boy's tombstone, and patted her little fingers on the smooth cold granite. She looked up at Grant. "Danny's my big brother now, isn't he?"

Jennifer blinked the tears from her eyes, and reached for her daughter. "Yes, he is, Pet.

How about we walk over and see the sailboats?"

As they left, she kissed Grant tenderly on the cheek. "It's good, Honey."

Alone now, Grant McKinnon went to one knee on the grass, and plucked at a weed growing among the shorn grass.

"Cathy. Sweetie," he whispered, "I am so sorry I wasn't there. Sorry for all the times I wasn't there." He bowed his head as the guilt took hold of him. Then, suddenly, he felt it drain out of him. "Never thought I'd find anyone else. Didn't really didn't want to. You were my first love. No one can take your place but... I have to go on. Make a good life again."

He looked over at Danny's grave. "Son, I love you and always will."

❋ ❋ ❋

In both Severodvinsk and Connecticut, warm breezes caught the men's words and lifted their messages up over the peaceful blue seas.

The End

About the Author

D. Clayton Meadows

D. Clayton Meadows served nearly twenty years on nuclear submarines. He served on the nuclear Fast Attack submarines USS RAY, USS DALLAS, and USS SPRINGFIELD. His writing includes the novel OF ICE AND STEEL, as well as numerous articles dealing with submarine history. He lives in Charleston, South Carolina.